Bascom ghosted through the woods. His passage was silent, disturbing nothing, leaving no trace. When he stopped, still as the trunk of a stout oak tree, he seemed to vanish into all that was around him.

Deep within the timber, a hundred yards or more from the creek, he suddenly went still. Far downstream his eye was drawn to the glint of sun on metal. Then, off in the distance, a bluejay sent up a scolding cry, echoing through the woods. He waited, certain the glint of metal was from saddle rigging or a horse's bit, something man-made.

Finally, at least a quarter-mile downstream, he saw movement. There was no need to wait longer, or see more.

Falling back into the woods, Bascom turned and raced toward his horse. He cursed himself for the fact that Luther Hall had caught him out. He told himself that the easy way out of Indian Territory hadn't worked. Now there was nothing left but the other way. The hard way.

## ST. MARTIN'S PAPERBACKS TITLES
## BY MATT BRAUN

# WESTWARD
## of the LAW

### MATT BRAUN

St. Martin's Paperbacks

WESTWARD OF THE LAW

Copyright © 1991 by Matt Braun.

ISBN: 0-312-93818-7
EAN: 9780312-93818-5

Printed in the United States of America

Bull Durham edition published 1991
St. Martin's Paperbacks edition / March 2006

St. Martin's Paperbacks are published by St. Martin's Press, 175 Fifth Avenue, New York, NY 10010.

10  9  8  7  6  5  4  3  2  1

# ONE

"Queens bet a dollar."

Tom Pryor studied the other man's hand. On the table was a queen-eight-queen-deuce. He figured it for two pair, probably queens and deuces. All afternoon he'd had miserable luck, pulling decent cards only to have them topped by better cards. He pondered a moment longer.

The other players had dropped out, and Newt Bascom was watching him with a blank expression. Pryor's own hand revealed a four-queen-ace-four. In the hole he had another ace, but it was the queen that gave him confidence. With three on the board, his opponent would have to hold the case queen in order to win. The odds dictated otherwise, and that prompted a sudden decision. He smiled.

"You bluffin' again, Newt?"

Bascom worked his chaw. He leaned sideways and centered a perfect hit on a nearby spittoon. "One way to find out," he said, with a delicate swipe at his mustache. "Call me and see."

"Hell with callin'!" Pryor peeled greenbacks off

his dwindling stack. "Your dollar and raise a dollar."

Bascom considered briefly, then shrugged. "Up another dollar."

"Suppose I just take the last one . . . a dollar more."

Without hesitation, Bascom matched the raise and nodded. "You're called."

"Read 'em and weep." Pryor grinned, flipped his hole card. "Two pair, aces and fours."

"Not quite good enough."

Bascom slowly turned his hole card, and Pryor found himself staring at three queens. His grin dissolved into a look of disbelief, then anger. He whacked the table with the flat of his hand. "Judas Priest! You caught the gawddamned case queen.

Bascom leaned forward to rake in the pot. His mustache lifted in a jocular smile. "Guess a little luck goes a long ways."

"Little luck, hell! I ain't never seen nothin' like it."

Sam Jordan, Bascom's partner, watched the exchange with an amused look. He creased a cigarette paper and sprinkled tobacco into it from a muslin bag of Bull Durham. After returning the bag to his shirt pocket, he deftly rolled the paper tight, licked the loose flap, and sealed the cigarette. He popped a match on his thumbnail, lit up in a haze of smoke, and inhaled deeply. Exhaling, he idly wondered why Pryor didn't call it a day, and cut his losses.

The game had started early that afternoon. For almost four hours, Bascom had been a consistent winner. The other men never knew whether he was bluffing, or actually held good cards. He seemed unbeatable.

Outside, the sun had heeled over to the west. Fading light from the front window of the saloon left the interior bathed in shadow. A cider glow spilled down on the table from an overhead lamp. One of the other players collected the cards and began shuffling.

The saloon was the second largest building in Tascosa. An isolated trading post, the town was situated on the Canadian River, little more than a way station in the vast emptiness of the Texas Panhandle. Apart from a few adobes, there was a general store and the saloon. Tascosa had no streets, only a handful of permanent residents, and no law. The nearest community of any size was a two-day ride south.

Joe Tate, who owned the saloon, stood behind the bar polishing glasses. His only customers were the five men seated around the poker table. The saloon was a crude affair, with a rough plank bar and tables along one wall. Still, it was the single saloon in the immense stretch of land separating Indian Territory from the eastern border of New Mexico. He had a corner on the liquor trade.

Scarcely two years ago there had been no trade of any nature. In the fall of 1874, General Ranald Mackenzie and his cavalry units had delivered a series of punishing defeats to the Southern Plains Tribes. The Comanche, who had ruled the Staked Plains from horseback, were ultimately driven onto the reservation. Since then, large cattle outfits had formed throughout the region, and now occupied the whole of the Texas Panhandle.

The five men at the poker table were, in one fashion or another, involved in the cattle business. Tom Pryor and his two friends were cowhands for the Slash O, a large spread along the western reaches of the Canadian. The other two men, Newt Bascom and Sam Jordan, were range detectives, sometimes known as regulators. Former cowhands themselves, they now worked for the Panhandle Cattlemen's Association. In a land where there was no law, their job was to put the damper on cattle rustlers and horse thieves. They were empowered to capture or kill anyone who stole live-stock.

To their friends, Jordan and Bascom were joshingly known as "The Durham Brothers." Jordan smoked Bull Durham roll-your-owns, and Bascom chewed plug tobacco of the same brand. One was seldom seen without a cigarette and the other always had a chaw working. Partners for many years, they had ridden for large cattle spreads throughout Texas. Then, not quite two years ago, they had been hired on as range detectives. There was no actual training for the job, but such men had to know cattle and not be averse to tangling with outlaws. They qualified on both counts.

Jordan was tall and solidly built, with piercing blue eyes and a thatch of chestnut hair. A cowhand since he was fifteen, and now barely thirty-two, he'd educated himself by reading everything from the Bible to the history of Rome. Though quiet and unassuming, he was nonetheless respected as a tough man, chain-lightning with his fists. He was also quick with a gun, and a deadly shot.

By contrast, Bascom was whipcord-lean with weathered features, dark hair, and an unruly mustache. His education was that of the land and of creatures; he was a superb tracker and a master of the wilderness. A man of ribald humor, his tastes ran to dance hall girls and any known form of gambling. Though no slouch with a gun or his fists, he preferred to outwit the other fellow whenever possible.

As range detectives, Jordan and Bascom had no other duties than to chase thieves. Often they were gone for weeks at a time, tracking outlaws wherever the trail led. Theirs was a hazardous profession, and they were reputed to have killed eleven hard cases who refused to surrender. But when they weren't on the trail, their time was their own, and they were at liberty to spend it however they saw fit. During their off-time, they could generally be found at Joe Tate's saloon.

Watching them now, Tate thought there might be trouble. Jordan was holding his own in the game, dragging down an occasional pot. Newt Bascom, on the other hand, was working on a winning streak that defied all odds. The problem was not that Bascom won too often, but rather that he'd won too much. Tom Pryor and the other cowhands earned thirty a month and found roughly a dollar a day. All three had close to a month's wages in the game, and most of it on Bascom's side of the table. Big losers, Tate knew from experience, were often sore losers.

One of the cowhands was dealing now, and the game was five-card draw. Bascom took a peek at his hand and discovered two pairs, kings and tens. Across the table, Pryor grunted to himself, holding three sevens. Pryor opened for a dollar, which was the limit they'd set at the start of the game. Bascom raised, and Pryor returned the favor. When Bascom took the last raise, Jordan and the other cowhand tossed in their cards.

On the draw, Bascom took one card and Pryor took two. The dealer took three cards, hoping to better a pair of jacks. Pryor bet, Bascom raised, and the dealer folded. A barrel-gutted man, with muddy eyes and a face pebbled with deep pockmarks, Pryor wouldn't back off. He hadn't improved his three of a kind, but he figured Bascom for two pair. He raised another dollar, and Bascom finished it with a third raise. His expression almost apologetic, Bascom spread his cards on the table. He'd caught a full house, tens over kings.

Pryor's face mottled with rage. He threw his cards down, glaring across the table. "You're one lucky sonovabitch, ain't you?"

"Don't take it personal," Bascom said, pulling in the pot. "Win some, lose some."

"Yeah, 'cept you don't never seem to lose."

"You got any complaints, talk to your pardner. He was dealin'."

"Mebbe so," Pryor growled. "'Course, you might've had that third ten up your sleeve."

Bascom started out of his chair. Jordan stopped him with a sudden motion, and fixed Pryor with a hard look. "You're liable to start something you can't finish. Everybody knows Newt's not a cheat."

Pryor barked a hollow laugh. He figured Jordan wouldn't pull a gun unless someone else pulled first. He figured as well that his bunkmates would back his play. Which made it good odds, three to two.

"Hold on there!" Joe Tate yelled from the bar. "Anybody spoilin' for a fight, take it outside."

The others were momentarily distracted. Pryor suddenly kicked back his chair and upended the table onto Bascom and Jordan. Bascom went over backwards, but Jordan shoved the table aside and stepped clear. One of the cowhands launched a looping haymaker, and he bobbed under the punch. Quick as a cat, he delivered a splintering combination, left hook followed by a murderous right. The cowhand went down as though he'd been poleaxed.

Pryor leaped over the table and jumped Bascom just as he stumbled to his feet. Jordan started to intervene, then caught a roundhouse to the jaw from the other cowhand. Knocked sideways, he regained his balance and shifted into a fighting stance. Out of the corner of his eye, he saw Vern Hungate, one of the hands on the Bar B spread, step through the door. He dodged and weaved a flurry of punches, waiting for an opening.

Bascom managed to squirm from underneath Pryor, and finally climbed to his feet. His nose was dripping blood and a welt had already formed over his left eye. As Pryor rose from the floor, Bascom waded in, hammering hard blows to the gut. Pryor's mouth ovaled in a woofing sound, and he doubled at the waist. Setting himself, Bascom put his weight into a sharp straight right to the chin. Pryor crashed backwards into the bar and Tate hit him over the head with a bung starter. He dropped to his knees, then pitched forward onto his face.

Still slipping punches, Jordan at last got an opening. He snapped a left, doubled with a hook, and followed with a clobbering overhand right cross. The cowhand shivered under the impact of the blow, then his eyes went blank and he toppled forward like a felled tree. Jordan stepped out of the way as the cowhand slammed into the floor. Breathing heavily, he turned to look at Bascom.

"You awright, Newt?"

"I'll live," Bascom said, wiping blood from his nose. "Just remind me not to play cards with that peckerhead no more."

Jordan's gaze shifted to the door. "Vern, why didn't you pitch in and lend a hand?"

Vern Hungate offered an elaborate shrug. "Wasn't my fight, Sam. Besides, didn't look like you needed no help, nohow."

"Well, something must have brought you here. What the hell you want?"

"Don't want nothin'," Hungate said. "The boss sent me to fetch you and Newt."

"Blalock sent you?" Bascom looked interested. "That mean we got a new assignment?"

"Beats me, Newt. He just told me to find you."

Jordan started toward the door. "Let's get a move on then."

Bascom rapidly collected a stack of greenbacks

from the litter on the floor. On his way past the bar, he nodded to Joe Tate. "Much obliged for the assist."

"Anytime a'tall, Newt. Always did hate a sore loser."

# TWO

The Canadian wound eastward with serpentine twists and turns. Jordan and Bascom, accompanied by Vern Hungate, rode silently along the river into the deepening nightfall. For a while, after leaving Tascosa, they had rehashed the saloon brawl. A good fight, they all agreed, made for lively sport. So long as no one got seriously damaged.

Bascom's nose had stopped leaking blood, and he was never one to hold a grudge. He was generally lucky at cards, whatever the game, and he understood how other men resented a heavy winner. He even accepted the gambler's maxim that a good loser was usually a regular loser. Yet he thought Tom Pryor had shown poor judgment, not to mention a lack of character. Only a hammerhead started a fight over a bad run of cards.

"Sorry sonovabitch," he said, almost to himself. "Oughta be a law against people like Pryor playin' poker."

Jordan chuckled. "Why hell, Newt, you looked like you were enjoying yourself. Leastways, it worked out once you got yourself untangled from him and that table."

"Gawdalmighty!" Bascom shook his head, laughing. "You see the pounding I give his gut? Bastard won't piss straight for a week."

"Yeah, you're a regular buzz saw once you come unwound."

Bascom shifted his chaw to the off-cheek. "You makin' fun of my pugilistic ability?"

"Not me, Newt. I'll hold your coat any day."

Bascom snorted, and they once again fell silent. Jordan pulled out the makings and rolled himself a cigarette. He struck a match on the saddle horn, cupping the flame in his hand, and puffed smoke. Off to the east, a full moon slowly arced higher in the sky. All around them the plains were lighted in a sallow glow.

Unbidden, a thought passed through his mind. He recalled another moonlit night, when he and Bascom had first seen the Texas Panhandle. Alex Blalock, after establishing the Bar B on the banks of the Canadian, had summoned them from south Texas. They had worked for him when he operated a spread along the Rio Grande. But he'd sold out the fall of '74, drawn north by the lure of virgin grasslands.

Before winter, Blalock had trailed a cattle herd into the Panhandle; a main house and outbuildings were raised, and he'd attracted top hands by paying top wages. Not long afterward, Colonel Charles Goodnight had established a ranch to the south of the Bar B, along the eastern rim of Palo Duro Canyon. With Blalock's operation thriving, and

Goodnight running close to 80,000 head, other cattlemen were shortly attracted to the Panhandle.

Once the Plains Tribes were herded onto the reservations in Indian Territory, thus removing the last obstacle to settlement, there had been a sudden influx of ranchers. Over the last year four cattlemen had organized large spreads around the Bar B boundaries, and Blalock had been instrumental in forming the Panhandle Cattlemen's Association. Since it was his idea, the other ranchers had voted him into office as president. Blalock was convinced that, with a spirit of cooperation, all would prosper equally along the Canadian.

In that, Jordan heartily agreed. After the chaparral and mesquite thickets of the Rio Grande, the boundless plains of the Panhandle were a cattleman's paradise. There were vast tracts of graze-land laced by streams feeding into the Canadian—sweet grass and clear water, everything western stockgrowers envisioned for a cattle spread. What all men sought, Alex Blalock had found in the Panhandle.

Tonight, riding toward the Bar B headquarters, Jordan was reminded that much had been accomplished in a brief span of time. Under the bright moon, everywhere he looked there were cattle standing hock-deep in lush graze, with a bountiful supply of water flowing endlessly eastward along the Canadian. The one fly in the ointment was an equally bountiful supply of rustlers and horse thieves. Wherever cattlemen prospered, thieves prospered as well. For those who preferred stealing to an honest day's labor, the open range was easy pickings.

In the beginning, Jordan hadn't been all that certain about working as a range detective. Granted, he and Bascom had served with the Texas volunteer cavalry toward the end of the Civil War. They had had permanent assignment as scouts, always well out front of their unit. By the summer of 1865, when the Union troops officially occupied the Rio Grande, they were seasoned veterans of the killing ground. Each wounded in separate engagements, both men had lost the queasy sensation that came on spilling another man's blood. War had taught them many things.

Yet the heat of battle was far different than tracking men down. And despite the impressive title, a range detective was more aptly dubbed by what the job required—manhunter. Along with tracking skills and a steady gun hand, the work demanded persistence and a certain amount of guile. Deception wasn't Jordan's strong suit, or Newt's either, and he had no knack for turning the other cheek. If someone rubbed him the wrong way, he usually settled it on the spot and pondered the wisdom of it later. With outlaws, of course, that wouldn't work. He'd learned to hold his temper in check and play whatever role suited the situation. One unguarded moment, even the simplest lapse, and a manhunter quickly lost the edge. Faced with a stiff rope, or a long prison sentence, those outside the law were prone to shoot first.

All of which made for a dicey proposition—one with long odds and damned little room for error. A range detective had to adapt to the moment, learn the tricks and dodges of those who rode the owlhoot trail. Otherwise, his life span would be shortened considerably.

Still, he and Newt had taken to the job like a couple of pups with a new bone. What they'd learned as scouts during the war had served them well in hunting men. The work was dangerous, but it beat the hell out of punching cows for a living. The pay was better, too. Far better. The Association wasn't stingy when it came to tracking down thieves.

Off in the distance, Jordan spotted a glimmer of light from the ranch compound. He took a drag on his cigarette, exhaling slowly, and wondered where the new assignment would lead. Not that it mattered to any great extent. One job was pretty much like another.

All operations for the Bar B were conducted from a headquarters compound located on a broad plain. The buildings were ranged along the south bank of the Canadian and formed an irregular oval beyond the main house. Aside from corrals and sheds, there were outbuildings for blacksmithing, carpentry, and general storage. A large bunkhouse, flanked by a combination kitchen and dining hall, was situated opposite the supply commissary.

Shaded by cottonwoods, the main house overlooked the river. Built after the fashion of a hacienda, it was a vast sprawl of adobe, with thick walls and deep-set windows. Hewn rafters protruded from the flat roof and the front door, wide and tall, stood like a fortress gate. A galleried ve-

randa, deeply shaded during the day, ran the length
of the front wall. The house was solidly constructed,
cool in the summer and warm in the winter.

Alex Blalock was waiting for them in his study.
The Bar B owner was short and bowlegged, but a
man of considerable stature astride a horse. He
knew cattle and he understood how to get the most
out of cowhands. On horseback or on foot he was a
commanding figure, and his authority was absolute
across his land. His hair was gray, and age lined his
face, but no one misread that for weakness. His
word was law on the Bar B.

A gruff man by nature, Blalock was nonetheless
partial to Jordan and Bascom. He'd known them
since the old days on the Rio Grande, and he respected them as he did few other men. Though he'd
never told them, he often thought they were cut
from the same bolt of cloth as himself. They were
hard and tough, and never accepted offense from
any man. Which was why he'd hired them to enforce
the law in a land that was westward of the law.

Tipped back in a leather judge's chair, he smiled
broadly as they entered the room. "Well, at last, the
wandering Durham Brothers."

"Like I always say," Jordan noted, "good for a
quarter-mile."

The remark was more fact than jest. In the early
days on the frontier, Bull Durham had been used as
a practical means of land measure. The buyer and
seller would build roll-your-owns, light up their cig-
arettes, and start riding. When they finished their
smokes, the distance marked was commonly ac-

cepted as a quarter-mile. No one questioned the length of a Bull Durham.

"Have a seat," Blalock said. "Take a load off your feet."

Jordan and Bascom settled into chairs directly in front of Blalock's broad walnut desk. Bascom took the chair nearest the spittoon, placed there for his benefit. Jordan began building himself a smoke.

"We got trouble," Blalock said in a rough voice. "Somebody stole that prize bull off the Circle I."

The statement caught Jordan in the midst of striking a match. He paused, the match flaming brightly, surprise written across his face. Hastily lighting the cigarette, he exchanged a look with Bascom, who appeared equally astounded. Bascom knuckled his mustache.

"Hell of a note," he said in wonderment. "Nobody ever stole a bull before."

Jordan exhaled a wad of smoke. "Christ, I'll go you one better. Why would anybody rustle a *bull*?"

Blalock grunted. "Simplest reason on earth. The critter's worth five thousand, maybe more."

"C'mon now," Bascom said in disbelief. "You sayin' Ingram paid five thousand dollars for a bull?"

"Bet your ass," Blalock countered. "Stanley Ingram don't do nothin' halfway. Goddamn critter was a Durham, imported all the way from England."

Longhorn cows were range animals, with more muscle than fat. Texas ranchers were all too aware that their stock lacked bulk and produced low-grade beef. Over the past year cattlemen had begun importing foreign bulls, with massive frames, in an effort to upgrade their herds. Lord Stanley Ingram, a transplanted British noble, was the first to try the experiment in the Panhandle.

Jordan took a long drag on his cigarette. "Don't make sense," he said, the words wrapped in smoke. "Foreign bulls aren't all that common. Besides which, even with the same breed, no two of them look exactly alike."

"Sam's right," Bascom observed. "After you stole the critter, who would you sell it to? Anybody with cow sense would spot a bull like that."

There was a moment of thoughtful silence. The three men pondered the question, but no ready answer presented itself. Foreign bulls, particularly in the land of longhorns, drew attention. Durham bulls, because of their unique conformation and general scarcity, were even more readily identifiable. Where would the thief sell such a bull?

"Get on it," Blalock ordered. "Ingram sent word the bull was stole last night. First thing tomorrow mornin', you go talk to him. Whoever did it, I want the bastard caught—*muy pronto*!"

Jordan and Bascom headed toward the bunkhouse. They had their orders and they knew Alex Blalock expected quick results. Whenever he used the words *muy pronto*, it was a signal to those who understood his character. No excuses would be tolerated.

Get the job done!

# THREE

**L**lano Estacado. The Staked Plains were a vast tableland. Flat and featureless, they stretched from eastern New Mexico into the Texas Panhandle. A brooding loneliness hung over *Llano Estacado* and, like an emerald ocean, buffalo grass and mesquite rippled on forever. Nothing changed as far as the eye could see.

Here and there, however, the plains were broken by canyons. Jordan and Bascom sat staring into one now, their horses drawn to a rein. They had departed the Bar B before first light, headed south, and a noonday sun marked their arrival at the canyon. Jordan's roan gelding pawed at the earth and Bascom's buckskin nibbled the grass. Before them, the yawning abyss abruptly dropped off.

Palo Duro Canyon was a colossal fissure, gouged into the earth over eons. A hundred miles long and a thousand feet deep, the broad gorge was walled north and south by sheer palisades. Far below, a winding river traced the floor of the canyon, and on either side of the stream, the land was lush with graze. Herds of cattle were visible against the verdant grasslands.

Along the north wall, an ancient path dropped downward into Palo Duro. Jordan nudged his horse over the rimrock and began a slow descent on the narrow rocky trail. Bascom gave him a few yards lead, then reined his buckskin onto the path. Not two years ago, Palo Duro had been the wilderness domain of the Comanche tribe. In 1874, after descending the craggy escarpment, the 4th Cavalry Regiment had defeated the lords of *Llano Estacado*. The Comanche, led by Quanah Parker, were soon herded onto a reservation.

Now, Palo Duro was the domain of cattle barons. Charles Goodnight was a legend among westering men, one of a dying breed. In 1866, with his partner Oliver Loving, he had blazed the Goodnight-Loving Trail from Texas to the high plains of Wyoming. Later, after Loving's death, Goodnight found a new partner. John Adair was a landed Irish aristocrat, heir to a vast fortune. Investment in Western cattle ranches was an increasingly popular sideline for foreign entrepreneurs with substantial wealth. In honor of John Adair, and his money, the ranch was dubbed the JA.

Downstream, sharing Palo Duro with the JA, was the Circle I spread. Lord Stanley Ingram, like many foreign nobles, was enamored with the sweep and grandeur of the American West. A man of immense resources, with ancestral lands in the north of England, he was drawn by the challenge and the enormous profits to be made in Western ranching. He became aware of Palo Duro through a periodical article about the Goodnight-Adair partnership. A year ago he had purchased 300,000 acres along the eastern border of the canyon.

The payroll of the Circle I exceeded fifty cowhands. A score of line shacks and distant cow camps were strung out along the lower reaches of Palo Duro. The ranch headquarters itself resembled a settlement, with the compound overlooking a wide stretch of river. Ingram and his family occupied a two-story log house, while the bunkhouses and storage buildings were spread along the shoreline. Unlike John Adair, who entrusted operation of the JA to his Texican partner, Ingram had hired a seasoned foreman to run the Circle I. He oversaw the outfit, but his principal concern was with breeding. His goal was to improve the bloodline of the native Longhorns.

Jordan and Bascom found the Circle I owner overseeing the final days of spring roundup. Ingram sat stiffly erect in the saddle, and they noted that he still used English rig and gear. He was tall and leanly built, with fair hair and light gray eyes. As they rode up, he waved and greeted them by name, having met them when he'd joined the Cattlemen's Association. They reined to a halt beside his sleek chestnut gelding.

"Good afternoon, gentlemen," he said in his clipped, British tone. "I gather you received the news of my unfortunate loss."

"Yessir, we did," Jordan affirmed. "Sorry to hear about your bull."

"Thank you." Ingram appeared distracted, intently watching the dusty melee of men and bawling calves. "I must say, I never tire of observing their skill in working stock. Absolutely fascinating."

The detectives turned their attention in the direction of his gaze. Several hundred cows had been gathered on a holding ground near the river. There the calves were roped, quickly separated from a herd of protesting mothers, and dragged to the branding fire. Working in teams, the cowhands swarmed over each calf after it was thrown. One man notched its ear with a knife while another stepped forward with a white-hot iron, and moments later the calf scrambled away with the ⊥ brand on its flank. Outriders hazed the calves back to the herd.

Jordan and Bascom were no strangers to roundups. They saw the work as monotonous and exhausting, not even remotely fascinating. Though it was early June, the cowhands sweltered under a ball of fire that seemed centered over the canyon. Their normal workday was sunrise to sunset, and they were lucky to get a noon break. Looking on, the detectives felt no great sentiment for the old days. By comparison their lives were leisurely, if occasionally hazardous.

"Bloody marvelous," Ingram said, nodding his head. "But, then, I suppose it's all rather routine to you gentlemen."

"Not hardly," Bascom paused, squirting a nearby rock with tobacco juice. He motioned toward the branding fire. "You got yourself a real good crew. Slicker 'n greased owlshit."

Lord Ingram was constantly amazed by Westerners' inventive metaphors, and their curious juxtaposition of curse words. He smiled, committing the phrase to memory, and reined his horse downstream. "What say we have a look at the scene of the crime?"

Jordan and Bascom followed his lead. On the ride back to ranch headquarters, Ingram questioned them at length about their work. He seemed particularly absorbed with the capture of desperate men, and the ever present danger of a shoot-out. They got the impression that things were a bit more civilized in England.

Upon arriving at the compound, Ingram dismounted before a large barn. He led them inside, where stalls lined both sides of a corridor. As they walked toward the rear, he explained that he'd built the barn to house his blooded horses, also imported from England. He stopped at the last stall on the right and stared at it with a melancholy expression. A door on the far wall opened onto a corral outside.

"Well—" he said sadly. "We kept Homer enclosed here. Selected lady visitors were brought to him for breeding purposes."

"Homer?" Jordan asked dubiously.

"Why, yes," Ingram replied. "Named after Homer, the Greek poet—the Iliad and the Odyssey."

"Oh." Jordan swapped a puzzled look with his partner. "How'd they make off with Homer, just exactly?"

"I haven't the faintest idea. Of course, there is a gate in the outside corral. I rather suspect they led him through there."

Bascom blinked. "Your bull lets himself be led?"

"Just so," Ingram acknowledged. "You see, Homer has a ring through his nose. Once you attach a snap to the ring, he willingly follows you anywhere."

"Feller could get himself killed trying that with a longhorn. Shore made it easy for the rustlers."

Jordan smothered a smile. "Lord Ingram, we were told this happened night before last. Any of your boys try to raise sign?"

"Sign?"

"Yeah, you know, tracks—a trail."

"Indeed not," Ingram said forcefully. "You and Mr. Bascom are the professionals in such matters. I awaited your arrival."

"What about a description of, uh, Homer? Any unusual markings?"

"Well, of course, he was branded with the Circle I. Apart from that, I have a rather nice painting of Homer. I'm a bit of an artist, you see."

"Could we get a look at the painting?"

"By all means."

Ingram led the way to the house. On the wall of his study hung a watercolor of Homer, posed against a backdrop of the grassy canyon. The bull was typical of a shorthorn Durham, stout and beefy, built low to the ground, his coat somewhat reddish in color. One of his horns took a noticeable upward slant.

Jordan took out the makings. As he sprinkled tobacco into the paper, he studied the painting. "I'd say we won't have any trouble spottin' him. 'Specially with that slanty horn."

"For that matter," Ingram pointed to the label affixed to the muslin tobacco bag, "you have your own painting for ready reference. Bull Durham used a perfect rendition when they designed their label. Except for the curved horn, that might very well be Homer."

Jordan held out the tobacco sack. He and Bascom scrutinized the label, nodding their heads. They glanced at the painting, checking it against the label. Homer and his Bull Durham look-alike were definitely birds of a feather.

"Not to stray," Ingram said thoughtfully, "but I wonder, are you familiar with the origins of your tobacco?"

"Just little things," Jordan admitted. He tucked the bag in his shirt pocket and lit the cigarette. "What makes you ask?"

"One might say I'm a student of the brand. A natural interest, since my ancestral home is in Durham County. Situated in northern England, of course, bordering the North Sea."

"Does Durham County have anything to do with the tobacco?"

"After a fashion," Ingram said. "Actually, it's a rather interesting story."

Warming to the subject, Ingram proved to be a student of history as well. At the close of the Civil War, he explained, armies of the Union and the Confederacy were positioned around the town of Durham's Station, in North Carolina. During the military surrender, nearly 80,000 men were foraging for food and other basics. Durham's Station lay

squarely between the two armies, and a tobacco factory was only a hundred yards from the railroad de-
pot. Unlike other manufacturers, the owner first
flue-cured and then granulated Bright yellow-leaf
tobacco, the finest tobacco in the Old South. His entire stock was consumed by the troops of both
armies within days.

Shortly after the war ended, letters began pouring
into Durham's Station from mustered out soldiers
across the country. The demand for such fine tobacco was little short of incredible, which prompted
other manufacturers to label their product as
Durham. In order to distinguish his brand from the
others, the factory owner adopted a picture of a
Durham bull as his trademark. His inspiration came
from a jar of mustard made in Durham, England,
which depicted a bull on the label. The official
brand name was Genuine Durham Smoking Tobacco, but it became universally known as Bull
Durham. Over the next two decades Bull Durham
went on to become the world's best-known tobacco.
Smokers everywhere, from Wall Street financiers to
Western cowhands, would settle for nothing less.
Ultimately, with full justification, it was advertised
as The Standard of the World.

"As you can see," Ingram concluded, "being from
Durham County, and raising Durham stock, I was
quite fascinated by the story. Small world, what?"

"How about that, Newt," Jordan said, grinning.
"Bet the boys in the bunkhouse will think we're
telling 'em a whopper."

Bascom looked impressed. "Sounds like God's unvarnished truth to me."

"Indeed it is," Ingram agreed. "A rather intriguing piece of history, gentlemen."

Late that afternoon, after retracing their path up the escarpment, Bascom began scouting for sign on the tableland. The earth was yielding, and before sundown he cut the two-day-old tracks. Three men, mounted on steel-shod horses, leading a bull. Their direction was northeast, toward the Canadian.

# FOUR

The plains went from dusk to dark. Without light, there was no way to follow the tracks farther. Yet Bascom was satisfied, for the trail had never once deviated. The direction was northeast, on a line to intersect the Canadian. He marked in his mind their present position, a dry arroyo.

"Way it looks," he said to Jordan, "these birds are gonna hit the river somewheres around Red Deer Creek."

Jordan nodded. "We'll be on the trail at first light. How long you figure before we catch up with them?"

Bascom took a plug from his vest pocket and bit off a chunk. He gummed the chaw a moment, considering. Some miles back he'd found the spot at a timbered creek where the rustlers had camped yesterday morning. From the sign, they were holing up during part of the day and traveling late afternoon through the night. Which meant they were on the move even now.

"Them jokers got a problem," he said, working

his chaw. "That bull don't take to fast travel. So they're movin' at a walk, and mostly at night. I figger they'll hit Red Deer Creek not long after sunrise tomorrow."

"Sounds reasonable," Jordan said. "We ought to get there sometime around late afternoon. Question is, will they hole up that long?"

"I tend to doubt it. These boys know their business. They'll be on the move again."

"Wonder where they'll head?"

"Reckon we'll find out tomorrow."

Turning northwest, they rode toward the Bar B headquarters. By the time they stepped down outside the corral, the moon had crested the eastern horizon. They unsaddled, turning their horses into the corral, and walked up to the mess hall. The cook grudgingly put together a warmed-over supper.

Afterward, they went to the bunkhouse. Bascom began collecting their gear for the trail. Tracking rustlers often became a fast and furious business, requiring speed as well as freedom of action. As a result, rather than hauling along a packhorse, they preferred to travel light. Whatever would fit into their saddlebags was what they took along. Extra boxes of cartridges, dried fruit, hardtack, coffee beans and a small coffee pot were the bulk of their gear. Accomplished plainsmen and hunters, they were versed in living off the land. A spare change of clothes was stuffed into their bedrolls.

Their weapons were of a match. Long ago they had concluded that it made sense to carry the same types of guns. For openers, it eliminated the need to lug along cartridges of different caliber. That cut down on the weight, and in the heat of a shoot-out, allowed one to provide the other man with fresh loads. Jordan, being the better pistol shot, opted for the Colt .45 as the sidearm with the most punch. Bascom, who excelled with a rifle, had chosen the Winchester .44-.40 with leaf sights. So their weapons were exact duplicates, and interchangeable, if the situation demanded. The one difference was that Bascom carried his pistol in a cross-draw holster.

While Bascom loaded their saddlebags, Jordan got busy with a straight razor. He stripped to the waist before a line of washbasins on a table near the door. After lathering his face, he shaved with quick strokes, peering into a faded mirror tracked to the wall. Then he scrubbed his upper body with the soapy water, washing away an accumulation of sweat and grime, and toweled dry. Wetting his hair, he gave it a few licks with a comb and studied himself in the mirror. He thought he'd done a passable job.

Some of the men were loafing around the bunk-house. They watched with interest as he put on his best shirt and the hand-tooled boots generally reserved for dances and social occasions. Sandy Pruett, a top hand in the crew, winked at one of the other men. Then, craning his neck, he gave Jordan an elaborate inspection.

"Goldang," he said archly. "You shore got yerself all dandified, Sam. Gonna chase badmen in those duds, are you?"

Jordan ignored the comment.

"Naw," another man jibed. "He's fixin' to go courtin'. I disremember that filly's name, Sam. Gimme a little hint."

Jordan strapped on his gunbelt.

"Rebecca," Pruett answered for him. "Known to them that holds hands with her as Becky. Ain't that right, Sam?"

Jordan took his hat from a wall peg, casually dusted it off. At the door, he looked back with a sardonic smile. "You boys dream about it when you hit the hay tonight. And no funny business under the covers."

Bascom let go a belly laugh, still stuffing gear into his saddlebags. When Jordan went out the door, he glanced over at Pruett. "Just to keep your mind off temptation, lemme tell you what I heard today. You ever hear the story about how Bull Durham got its start?"

"Shit a brick!" Pruett moaned. "You done bent our ears out of shape with Bull Durham stories."

"Nothin' like what I'm gonna tell you now. You see, there's this place called Durham's Station back yonder in North Caroliny . . ."

Mounted on a fresh horse, Jordan made good time. Hardly more than an hour later, he dismounted in the yard of the Culpepper ranch. On the porch, seated in rockers, were Harry Culpepper and his wife. Jordan looped the reins around the hitch rack, then loosened the cinch on his horse. As he walked toward the house, he cursed under his breath. He'd hoped the Culpeppers would have been in bed by now.

"Evening, Harry," he said, remembering to doff his hat. "How do, Miz Culpepper."

"Tolerable," she replied in a huffy tone. "Little late to come calling, isn't it?"

"Yes, ma'am," Jordan conceded. "But I've got some work that'll keep me gone a while. Only found out about it today."

"Work!" she sniffed. "You're going to get yourself killed, you stay in that line of work. You ought to settle down to a regular job."

Jordan forced a smile. "Man does what he's good at, Miz Culpepper. Becky inside?"

"Stay where you are. I'll fetch her."

Naomi Culpepper rose from the rocker, which groaned under her weight. She was a ponderous woman, with lumpy breasts and widespread hips. By comparison, her husband was built like a fence post, and Jordan had always thought it a curious match. Still, it was revealing in other ways, especially where their daughter was concerned. Given time, the daughter would turn out very much like her mother. The image was never far from mind when he came calling.

"Hadn't heard nothin'," Harry Culpepper said as his wife entered the house. "Whose stock got rustled?"

"Somebody hit the Circle I. Got off with Lord Ingram's prize bull."

"Now ain't that a helluva note. Who'd steal a bull?"

"I'll let you know when I get back."

Culpepper was silent a moment. "The missus has a sharp tongue on her. But she's right, what she said about your work. Not much future in chasin' riffraff and such."

Jordan considered it same song, second verse. Every time he came to call, he got much the same lecture. The Culpeppers weren't worried about his personal well-being, and they had no moral objection to the idea of range detectives. On occasion, he and Newt had recovered stock rustled from their herd. What worried them was their daughter's prospects.

Neither of the Culpeppers believed that Jordan was interested in matrimony. He struck them as a roamer, a man who would never be tied down. They were desperate to marry off their daughter, for she was approaching twenty-three. Yet she seemed smitten with Jordan, and never exhibited interest in other men. Worse, were she to marry him, and he to get killed, they would have a young widow back on their doorstep. To them, there was no good side to the relationship.

Rebecca emerged from the door, framed in a spill of lamplight. She was a robust girl, with apple cheeks and deep-set dimples. Her hair was flaxen and golden curls spilled down over her forehead. As she crossed the porch, her gingham gown stretched tautly across her breasts, and Jordan felt a stirring in his loins. She was a looker, and wilder than her parents imagined.

"Good evening, Sam," she said engagingly. "Mama tells me you're off on the owlhoot again."

Jordan nodded. "Liable to be gone a spell. Thought I'd drop by and pay my respects."

"Daddy, Mama—" Rebecca stepped off the

porch—"would you excuse us? We'll take a walk down by the creek."

"Don't stray," Mrs. Culpepper said sternly from the door. "And don't stay too long, neither."

"Yes, Mama."

A brisk walk brought them to a creek south of the house. Huge live oaks sheltered the grassy bank, and for nearly a year, this had been their trysting place. She paused, Jordan beside her, broken moonlight filtering through the trees. Her face was radiant in the dappled glow, and eager.

Without a word, Jordan took her in his arms. She felt the corded strength of his body, and her arms circled his neck. He kissed her soundly, and her tongue playfully darted about his mouth. When they parted, her voice was husky.

"*Ummm.* That's what I call a real hello."

"Best there is," Jordan agreed. "'Course I couldn't hardly do that in front of your folks."

"God forbid!" she said quickly. "They already believe you're only interested in one thing. Mama's scared to death I'll get in a family way."

"You think they know?"

"Of course, silly. They probably did the same thing before they got married."

Lately, her hints about marriage had grown broader. Jordan chose to ignore them, and tonight was no exception. He casually motioned off into the distance. "I can't stay long. Have to be on the trail by daybreak."

Her face sobered. "Whenever you ride off, I get

sick at heart. Every night I say a prayer you'll come back safe."

"No need to trouble yourself. 'Case nobody ever told you, I lead a charmed life."

"I hope so, honey." She suddenly brightened. "You know, maybe you're right."

"What do you mean?"

"Well . . ." she vamped him with a look. "You charmed me right out of my pants, didn't you?"

"Yeah, I reckon so." Jordan grinned, cupped her chin in his hand. " 'Course, I don't recollect you tried to fight me off."

She laughed a deep throaty laugh. "Never have, never will. You're my man."

"Sure about that, are you?"

"One way to find out."

Jordan drew her into a close embrace. Her mouth met his greedily, and her tongue parted his lips, at once inviting and teasing. He lifted her in his arms, slowly lowered her to the grassy bank, and eased down beside her. A tangle of arms and legs, breathing hard, they came together in a frenzied clash. She began tugging at the buckle on his gun belt, then popped the buttons on his pants. Lost in the rush of the moment, his hand touched bare flesh, crept higher beneath her skirt. Her back arched and she hugged him tighter. Her mouth ovaled in a low moan.

Along the creek, the katydids fell silent.

# FIVE

Jordan and Bascom entered the mess hall an hour before first light. The cook, a taciturn man with no sense of humor, was grumpy but nonetheless obliging. He laid out a spread of beefsteak, fried eggs, sourdough biscuits, and a pot of strong coffee. Depending on where the trail would lead, this might be their last full meal in a long while.

The stars still flickered in a pale sky when they rode out. Jordan hadn't returned to the ranch until after one in the morning. At best, he'd caught three hours sleep before Bascom shook him awake. Yet he was alert and clear-eyed, apparently no worse for wear. He rolled himself a cigarette as they rode from the compound.

"You're lookin' right pert," Bascom commented. "Leastways for a feller that spent the night tomcattin' around the country."

Jordan lit up in a puff of smoke. "Lots of loving keeps a man young, Newt. I just suspect that's your problem."

"What problem's that?"

"Every mornin' you're grouchy as a bear with a sore tail. You need yourself a steady woman."

"Thanks all the same," Bascom mumbled. "I'll stick to catch as catch can."

Jordan chuckled. "One of these days those shady women are gonna give you a dose of you-know-what."

"Well, my tally-whacker ain't fell off yet. Besides, an ugly bastard like me don't have much choice when it comes to ring-dang-doo."

Jordan thought otherwise. Bascom was by no means a handsome man, but he wasn't homely either. He simply found sporting women preferable to those who comported themselves as ladies. Jordan often reflected that it was an offshoot of the many years Bascom had spent trailing cattle. Cowhands liked their women wild and bawdy, game for any kind of bedroom high jinks. Sentiment was seldom part of the bargain.

A few minutes before sunrise they arrived at the dry arroyo. Like following a map, Bascom had the spot firmly fixed in his head from last night. Long ago, he'd learned that a wilderness manhunt required patience. Any seasoned tracker always awaited sunrise before trying to cut sign.

On hard ground the correct sun angle often made the difference between seeing a print or missing it entirely. The tracker stationed himself so that the trail would appear directly between his position and the sun. In early morning, with the sun at a low angle, he worked westward of the trail. The easterly sunlight would then cast shadows across the faint imprints of man or horse.

A tracker seldom saw an entire footprint or hoofprint unless the ground was quite soft. On rocky terrain there was even less likelihood that complete prints would be spotted. What the tracker looked for instead were flat spots, scuff marks, and disturbed vegetation. Of all sign, flat spots were the most revealing.

Only hooves or footprints, something usually related to man, would leave flat spots. Small creatures might leave faint scuff marks or disturb pebbles. But a flat spot was unnatural to nature, whatever the type of terrain. There was never any doubt that it had been made by a hooved animal, or a man.

Bascom dismounted, handing the reins of his horse to Jordan. He then moved several paces west of the trail and squatted down on his haunches. The sun, flaming brightly on the horizon, sent shafts of light directly across the trail. His hat brim shaded his eyes, and the almost invisible imprints of three horses and a large hooved animal were cast in shadow by the sun. The direction, as though indicated by a compass needle, was northeast.

Still on foot, Bascom walked along the trail. A short distance from the arroyo, the earth became softer, stubbled with grass. Squatting down, he studied crushed patches of grass, irregular in shape but uniformly spaced, and all on a direct march to the northeast. Plain to read, three men mounted on horses were leading the bull at a walking pace.

Framed in a yielding spot of ground was the full im-
print of a horse's left forefoot. The metal shoe had a
chip in the rounded front edge.

Bascom stood, nodding back at Jordan. He
pointed at the track. "One of our boys has a horse
with a chink in his shoe. Sticks out like a diamond in
a goat's ass."

"Glad to hear it," Jordan said. "Won't leave any
room for argument once we nail him."

"Nope, no argument. I could track that jaybird
through a buffalo herd."

The sun rose higher as Bascom stepped into the
saddle. His gaze fixed on the trail, they rode off at a
ground-eating trot. Occasionally, he stopped to
study the tracks, but his inspection required little
calculation. The thieves were on a straight line.


Red Deer Creek bisected the Canadian. On the
south bank, the creek angled off to the southwest.
Across the river on the opposite bank, the stream
fed into the Canadian from the north. With spring
runoff now past, the river was easily fordable. The
creek, north and south, was less than three feet deep.

Jordan and Bascom dismounted where the southern tributary flowed out of the river. There, along the
timbered shoreline, they found the remains of a
campfire. Jordan kept the horses at a distance while
Bascom investigated the site. There were heel marks
from boots, and indications that the horses had been
hobbled on a grassy swale. The bull had been tied to
a tree, with enough slack to let it graze. Droppings
from all four animals littered the ground.

Bascom stuck his hand into the ashes of the campfire. Far down, there was a faint warmth, and he judged the fire had cooled for about three hours. He next moved to a pile of horse manure on the grassy swale. The droppings were dark and crusted, but still soft inside when punched with a stick. Only a few flies buzzed the droppings, and that was the best indication of age. The older the droppings, the fewer the flies.

The horse with the chipped shoe was evidenced from stampings in the earth. There were fresher tracks leading from the campsite to the south bank of the river. Bascom looked for the change of color caused by the dry surface of the earth having been disturbed to expose a moister, lower surface. Heat increased the rate at which tracks age, and the sun was now in the western quadrant. The undersurface of the hoofprints was all but restored to the normal color of the ground. Every sign indicated that the rustlers had departed camp somewhere around midday.

After he rejoined Jordan, they forded the river. They searched the north bank for the spot where the thieves had emerged from the water. The earth on the shoreline was undisturbed for a quarter-mile in either direction. Doubling back, they then rode the north fork of Red Deer Creek. A mile upstream they reined to a halt. Nowhere was there any sign leading from the creek.

"Shifty sonsabitches," Bascom muttered. "They took to the water and Christ knows where they come out. Could be headed any whichaways."

"No need to check the south fork," Jordan noted. "That heads right back the way we just come."

Bascom motioned off to the east. "Don't make much sense that they'd take the river downstream. Leads straight into Injun country."

Some miles to the east, the Canadian crossed the boundary line into Indian Territory. Jordan bobbed his head in agreement. "One thing's for sure," he said. "They wouldn't follow the river west from here. That'd take 'em back into the Panhandle."

"Trick like that would be crafty but downright dumb. And all the sign says these gents are nobody's fool."

"So where'd they disappear to?"

Bascom spat a thin stream of tobacco juice. He wiped his mustache and sat there with a faraway look. Jordan pulled out his Bull Durham, rolled himself a cigarette, and waited while his partner thought it out. Bascom finally wagged his head.

"Way it looks," he said, "these boys quit their camp around noontime. I allow they figgered to be bedded down somewheres about nightfall."

"You sayin' what I think you're sayin'?"

"Wish to hell I weren't."

The sun drifted westward as they reined their horses around. They rode north, toward No Man's Land.

Wild Horse Lake lay on the divide between the Beaver and the Cimarron Rivers. For centuries the Comanche and Kiowa had used it as a campsite during their fall hunts. But the Indians came here no longer. Nor were there any towns or ranches within a three-day ride. Wise men avoided this remote stretch of wilderness, for it was a place where neither God nor law was recognized. Judge Colt ruled supreme at Wild Horse Lake.

No Man's Land literally belonged to no one. Through a maze of obscure treaties, it was a raw expanse forgotten by God and government alike. Separated by Texas and Kansas for a depth of some thirty-five miles, it extended in a narrow strip nearly two hundred miles long. Indian Territory marked its eastern boundary, and its western reaches touched the borders of Colorado and New Mexico. In time, this isolated wilderness had become a sanctuary for killers and renegades of every stripe.

Not even U.S. Marshals dared venture into No Man's Land. For it was common knowledge that, while a lawman might ride in, he would never ride out. A man on the dodge could find no safer haven, and those who rode the owlhoot retreated there with no fear of pursuit. Whatever his crime, an outlaw found immunity at Wild Horse Lake.

The lake itself was actually a large basin. Somewhat like a deep bowl, it served as a reservoir for spring meltoff and the occasional thundershowers. Above the basin, sweeping away on all sides, was a limitless prairie where the grasses grew thick and tall. Dusk settled over the land as Jordan and Bascom lay hidden at the top of the basin. Their horses were ground-reined a hundred yards to the rear.

Jordan scanned the lake with a small brass telescope. Spotted around the broad shoreline were a dozen or more outlaw camps. The men who head-quartered here lived in a state of armed truce. By unwritten law, no one asked questions of a man from another camp. Smoke from cooking fires drifted skyward, and saddle horses were picketed near each campsite. Small herds of horses and cows, all stolen, were scattered around the basin.

"See anything?" Bascom asked.

Jordan lowered the spyglass. "Newt, that bull's not down there."

"Hell's bells, he's gotta be! Them boys was headed north."

"Maybe so, but they didn't stop off here."

"Then where the Christ are they?"

There was a moment of weighing and delibera-tion. At length, Jordan collapsed the telescope and shoved it into his pocket. He gestured off to the northeast. "That's the way they've been headed from the start. Straight as a string, and it ends at Dodge City."

"C'mon, Sam!" Bascom groaned. "Would you waltz a rustled bull into Dodge?"

"Well, it's a damn long ways from the Panhandle. 'Course, if you got any better ideas, I'm all ears."

Bascom stared down at the basin. "This here was my best idea."

Night fell as they rode out from Wild Horse Lake. Their bearing was the North Star, slightly north by northeast. Toward Dodge City.

# SIX

Three days later Jordan and Bascom sighted what was being touted as the Queen of Cowtowns. Their journey had taken them from No Man's Land across the boundless prairies of western Kansas. They were hot and tired, ready for a bath and a fresh change of clothes. Yet they operated on the principle of business before pleasure.

Dodge City sweltered under a midday sun as they rode into the South Side. Trailing season had begun in earnest, and the vice district was jammed with Texans. Upward of five hundred trail-weary men were in town at any given time, and a carnival atmosphere permeated the streets. Saloons and whorehouses and gambling dives lined the boardwalks, all catering to the rowdy nature of cowhands. A combination of wild women and popskull whiskey quickly separated most of them from their wages.

Dodge had only recently captured part of the cattle trade. Some cattlemen still drove their herds up the Chisholm Trail, to railhead at Wichita. But a great many Texans, since the expansion of railroads into western Kansas, now trailed their herds by a shorter route. The Western Trail began at Doan's Crossing on the Red River, meandered through Indian Territory, and ended at the Arkansas River, on the outskirts of Dodge. For some of the cowhands, particularly those from south Texas, the long trail to railhead exceeded a thousand miles. To them, the town was like an oasis at the end of a desert crossing.

Hammered together out in the middle of nowhere, Dodge had been transformed from a trading post for buffalo hunters into the rawest boomtown on the western plains. A sprawling, windswept hodgepodge of buildings, the town was neatly divided by the railroad tracks. The vice district, known simply as the South Side, was wide open, night and day. There, the trailhands were allowed to let off steam with raucous abandon, gunplay excepted. But at the railroad tracks, locally dubbed the Deadline, all rowdiness ceased. Anyone who attempted to hurrah the north side of town was guaranteed a stiff fine and a night in jail.

Upon crossing the tracks, it was like passing from a three-ring circus into a sedate churchyard. Along Front Street, the dusty plaza gave every appearance of a thriving little metropolis. Down at one end, flanked by a mercantile and several smaller establishments, were the Dodge House, Zimmerman's Hardware, and the Long Branch Saloon. Up the other way were a couple of trading companies and the bank, bordered by cafes and shops and varied business places. To the north was the residential section, and outside town vast herds of longhorns were being grazed along the winding Arkansas.

Everyone along Front Street conducted themselves in an orderly fashion. For the most part, they acted as though the South Side simply didn't exist. The arrangement was remarkable, even by Western standards, yet highly sensible. The wages of sin on one side of the tracks and the fruits of commerce on the other. The Deadline served as a neutral ribbon of steel in between. To the benefit of all concerned, it worked uncommonly well.

One of the major reasons for this success was the lawman who maintained order in Dodge City. Tales filtering back down the trail told of peace officers who were handy with their fists and quick with a gun. They rigidly enforced the Deadline, and any cowhand who ventured into the north side did so at his own risk. The trail crews were especially bitter toward the Deputy City Marshal, Wyatt Earp. Formerly a lawman in Wichita, Earp made no bones about his dislike of Texans in general, and cowhands in particular. In turn, they looked upon him as a blue-belly Yankee, the natural enemy of any true Texican. Given the slightest excuse, he took personal pleasure in busting their heads.

Jordan and Bascom were familiar with Earp's reputation. Though they had never crossed paths with him, he'd been on the police force the last time they trailed a herd to Wichita. Like all Texans, they had no great fondness for Yankees. In Earp's case, they had no respect for the man. During their brief stay in Wichita, they had heard tales about his background. Tales which no one disputed, including Wyatt Earp.

Northerners come west, the Earp family had settled around Wichita. There were four brothers all told, Wyatt being the most ambitious of the lot. They'd made a start on the frontier operating sleazy saloons and two-bit whorehouses. Court records in Wichita left no doubt that they had been fined for running unlicensed houses of ill repute. Then, through political connections, Wyatt had wrangled a job on the police force. He became a model of decorum, though his brothers still conducted business as usual. His attitude toward lawbreakers was much like the loathing a reformed drunk has for the local barfly. He regularly pounded skulls.

No one questioned Earp's courage. He was a tough, hard-fisted man, willing to wade into the thick of a saloon brawl. In Wichita, he became known for "buffaloing" cowhands, whacking them over the head with the barrel of his pistol. On occasion, he'd traded shots with the Texans, and newspapers reported that he had killed one man. Yet, despite his respectable front, he still associated with the sporting crowd. His closest friends were gamblers, confidence men, and a notorious mankiller, Doc Holliday. He'd never quite outdistanced his past, even though he now wore a badge. Word had it that he was secretly married to one of his former whores.

Anywhere in Texas, Jordan and Bascom were welcomed by the local peace officers. Though they were not sworn lawmen, the range detectives were respected throughout cattle country. They knew nothing of Dodge City, and the logical starting place for their investigation would be the marshal's office. Yet they were Texans, and they'd heard that Wyatt Earp was the chief deputy. The idea of asking help from someone they held in low regard grated on them all the more since they knew Earp's opinion of Texicans.

Across the railroad tracks, they asked directions from a passerby. The man pointed to a one-story building not far from the Long Branch Saloon. They dismounted outside the marshal's office, and left their horses tied to the hitch rack. Dusting themselves off, they trooped inside, all too aware of their grungy appearance. The interior was dim and cool, the windows shaded by a roofed porch.

Wyatt Earp sat behind a wooden desk. To his left was the door to the cell block and on the opposite wall was a gun rack with several carbines and sawed-off shotguns. He was much as they remembered him from their summer in Wichita. A man of medium height, solidly built, with thinning hair and a handlebar mustache. He was in shirtsleeves, a holstered Colt strapped onto his right hip. His eyes were cold.

As they entered, he looked up from a stack of paperwork. He gave them a quick once-over, and his expression turned dour. "What can I do for you?"

Jordan took the lead. "I'm Sam Jordan and this is Newt Bascom."

Earp nodded, staring at them.

"We're range detectives," Jordan went on. "Operate out of the Texas Panhandle."

"You have any papers to identify yourselves?"

"What kind of papers?"

"Commission papers," Earp said testily. "Something that proves you work for an association."

"Nope," Jordan replied. "No papers."

"Then how the hell do I know you're who you say you are?"

"Guess you'll just have to take our word. Where we come from, that's good enough."

Earp frowned. "You trying to get smart with me, mister?"

"Well, marshal," Jordan said flatly, "I reckon you can take it any way you please. I'm not accustomed to people questioning my word."

Earp stiffened in his chair. Their eyes locked, and Jordan held his gaze, clearly unimpressed. After a moment Earp became aware that he could take it the next step or let it drop. The Texan would accommodate him either way.

"State your business," Earp said crisply. "I haven't got all day."

"Like I said, we're from the Panhandle. We're chasin' a couple of rustlers that stole a prize bull."

"What kind of prize bull?"

Jordan hauled out his Bull Durham sack. He held it out, indicating the label. "Looks exactly like that one, a Durham bull. Imported from England."

Earp glanced at the tobacco sack, and his eyes narrowed. "You trying to pull my leg, mister? I never heard of a bull like the one on Bull Durham."

"Gospel truth," Bascom interjected. "Copied that bull off an English mustard jar, right after the War

Between the States. We got it straight from the horse's mouth."

"Who might that be?"

"Lord Stanley Ingram, down Palo Duro way. His bull's the one that got stole."

Earp looked from one to the other. Finally, he shook his head. "All right," he said. "Anybody with that story has to be on the square. What do you want from me?"

Jordan began rolling a cigarette. "We think the rustlers were headed for Dodge. We've never been here before, and we don't know the layout." He paused to lick the paper, then struck a match and lit up. "Thought you might be able to put us on the right track."

"Are you asking me if I've seen that bull?"

"Nooo," Jordan said slowly. "I'm asking you who around here would handle rustled stock."

Earp scowled. "You're not saying I'd have any truck with rustlers—are you?"

"Marshal, you're the law hereabouts. Only figures you'd know who's got dirty hands and who don't."

"Well—" Earp considered a moment. "There's one fellow, a livestock dealer by the name of George Goddard. Understand, it's only rumor. We've never caught him at anything."

"Thank you, kindly," Bascom said quickly. "We'll have ourselves a talk with him. Might just be our man."

"You listen close," Earp said in a hard tone. "We don't tolerate Texas justice in Dodge. You take my meaning?"

Jordan looked at him. "What is it you call 'Texas justice'?"

"Way I hear it, you range detectives hang them first and ask questions later. You try that around here and your ass is mine."

"Newt and me never yet hung anybody. We'll send you a personal invite first time we do."

Earp leaned forward in his chair. "Just remember what I told you. One warning's all you get."

Jordan smiled. "Appreciate the tip, marshal. You've been a big help."

They left Earp staring nails as they went out the door. On the boardwalk, Bascom let out a deep breath. He glanced sideways at Jordan.

"You're a regular goddamn rooster, aren't you? Why'd you have to push him so hard?"

Jordan took a drag on his cigarette. "Bastard rubbed me the wrong way." He exhaled smoke with a wide grin. "Ought to have more respect for Texicans."

"Christ on a crutch!" Bascom groaned. "Try honey sometime. Works lots better than vinegar."

"Why hell, Newt, you're slick talker enough for both of us."

Still grumbling, Bascom led the way to the hitch rack. They mounted their horses and rode off down the street. Now that they had a name, they knew where to start. On the South Side, where the livestock dealers were.

# SEVEN

Across the Deadline, Jordan and Bascom skirted the train station. They held their horses to a walk, scanning the cluster of buildings ranged eastward along the railroad tracks. Toward the end of town, near the cattle pens and loading yard, was a livery stable. A sign atop the structure also identified the proprietor as a livestock dealer.

Bascom worked his cud. "How we gonna play this?"

"Slow and easy," Jordan said. "Act like we're fresh off the trail and looking for jobs."

"You talkin' about honest jobs?"

"Yeah, we'll start that way. Then we'll ease around to the subject of night work. See how he takes the bait."

"What if he don't?" Bascom asked. "Take the bait, I mean."

Jordan smiled. "Then we'll try the other way."

The statement required no elaboration. Jordan was tough and pragmatic where lawbreakers were

concerned. His code was the end justified the means
with men who operated windward of the law. Since
thieves followed no rules, he played the game ac-
cordingly, with a slight variation. He wrote his own
rules as he went along.

Bascom was of a similar mind. Given a choice,
he would have stuck to the letter of the law. But his
experience as a detective had convinced him that the
law applied only to the law-abiding. Those men who
rode the owlhoot ignored all laws, whether devised
by God or man. That being the case, any dealings
with them became elemental in nature. If the easy
way wouldn't work, the hard way usually would. He
figured they deserved whatever they got.

Outside the livery stable, they dismounted and
left their horses tied to the hitch rack. Walking
through the broad double doors, they paused and inspected the row of stalls on either side of the building. The place was filled with a regular rainbow of
odors—old leather, hay and fresh droppings—
blended into a pleasant, musklike aroma. Except for
the stalled horses, and a stablehand shoveling manure, the livery appeared deserted.

A door opened, leading from an office on the left,
and a man hurried forward. He wore matching
trousers and vest, with a starchy white shirt, and a
gold watch chain dangled across his paunch. From
all appearances, it seemed unlikely he'd be caught
tending stables. He stopped, nodding amiably,
thumbs hooked in his vest.

"Afternoon, gents. What can I do for you?"

Jordan took the lead. "You the boss hereabouts?"

"George Goddard's the name. In the market for a horse, are you?"

"Not just exactly." Jordan feigned a sheepish look. "We come up with a trail herd couple of days ago. Got busted out at the card tables."

"How's that involve me?"

"Well, we're lookin' for work. Long ways back to Texas with empty pockets."

"Damn bet'cha!" Bascom chimed in. "Any sorta job would do. We ain't particular."

Goddard frowned. He'd seen dozens like them over the past two trailing seasons. Cowhands hired on for the drive north, then paid off once the herd reached railhead. How they got back to Texas, or when, was their own lookout. Those who went broke at the gaming dives and cathouses faced especially bleak prospects. They needed a stake to outfit themselves for the long ride south.

"Sorry, boys," Goddard said, motioning back at his stablehand. "I've got all the help I can use."

Jordan and Bascom followed the direction of his gaze. Outside, through a rear door, there was a large stock pen, built to hold fifty head or more. But today something less than thirty horses stood munching hay scattered across the ground. The animals were of mixed coloring and bore a variety of brands. From what Wyatt Earp had said, some of them might well be stolen. There was no way to tell without tracing the brands through livestock records.

"What about them ponies?" Jordan inquired. "Any of them need some extra work? We're good with broncs."

"Not in that bunch," Goddard said. "I only trade in well-broke saddlestock. Ranchers up north won't buy nothing else."

"Up north?"

"Wyoming and Montana."

Jordan gave him a quizzical look. "Thought that was Sioux country."

Goddard chuckled softly. "You boys ought to read the newspapers. The army's got a campaign underway to whip those red heathens once and for all."

"That a fact?"

"I'm here to tell you it's a fact. Why, just yesterday, I read that General Custer would be commanding the 7th Cavalry. Sioux and the Cheyenne won't know what hit 'em!"

"Now that you mention it," Bascom noted, "I heard tell lots of cowmen were startin' outfits on the High Plains. Appears they think Custer will put them Injuns to rout."

"I'm banking on it," Goddard informed him. "Within the year, that'll be the biggest market for horseflesh in the world."

"Sounds like you figger to cash in on it."

"Supply and demand, that's the name of the game! I plan to supply all they'll buy."

There was something of the charlatan about Goddard. His voice had the broad exaggeration of a man hawking snake-oil liniment from the tailgate of a torch-lit wagon. He rocked back on his heels, thumbs in his vest pockets, looking pleased with himself.

Jordan pointed out the back door. "You'd better get busy if you're fixin' to supply all that demand.

What you got in your corral wouldn't hardly stock a small outfit."

"Lots of horses around," Goddard said smugly. "No worries on that score."

Jordan exchanged a covert glance with Bascom. Then he moved closer to Goddard, lowering his voice. "Listen here, how'd you like to get some cow ponies real quick, real cheap?"

Goddard eyed him with a keen, sidewise scrutiny. "What's that supposed to mean?"

"Well, me and my partner"—Jordan hooked a thumb at Bascom—"we've done a little night work in our time. Horses, cows, it don't make no nevermind to us. Whatever you want, we'll deliver."

"I don't deal in cattle."

"So we'll stick to horses."

A moment of deliberation slipped past. Goddard's eyes narrowed, and he inspected them with open calculation. Finally, he shook his head. "Thanks all the same, boys. I think I'll pass."

"Hell's fire!" Bascom blurted. "We gotta raise a stake somehow. We're busted flat!"

Jordan nodded agreement. "Look here," he said to Goddard, "why not put us in touch with whoever does your work now? We'll ride for them."

"Whoa there," Goddard said in an offended voice. "Nobody ever yet accused me of dealing in suspect stock."

"What the hell," Jordan said, mugging a sly smile. "We'll keep it our little secret."

"Whoever you boys are, you'd better be on your way. I don't much care for this conversation."

Jordan took out the makings. He rolled a cigarette, then lit up and snuffed the match. He held out the Bull Durham bag, indicating the label. His smile suddenly turned cold.

"See that bull?"

Goddard stared at the label. "What about it?"

"We're in the market for one. English bull, called a Durham. We'd pay good money, and throw some your way too. All you have to do is put us on the right track."

"Get out of here!" Goddard said indignantly. "And don't let the door hit you in the ass!"

"You're sure about that?" Jordan said.

"Damn good and sure. Go on—git!"

Jordan stuck the cigarette in the corner of his mouth. His fist lashed out and he punched the livestock dealer in the belly. Goddard's mouth popped open in a whooshing sound and his eyes bulged like glittery marbles. He sank slowly to his knees, gulping for breath.

The stablehand turned from a stall at the rear, his expression alarmed. Then, hefting his shovel like a club, he started forward. Bascom drew his pistol and casually wagged it in the stablehand's direction. His voice was pleasant, but firm.

"Suppose you have a seat and watch the fun."

The stablehand obediently seated himself on the floor. While Bascom covered him, Jordan turned back to Goddard. He squatted down face-to-face with the livestock dealer, and dangled the Bull Durham sack at eye level. "Let's try again," he said. "Tell me the name of somebody with a bull like that."

Goddard sucked in air. "Told you," he sputtered. "Don't deal in cattle."

"Just stolen horses—right?"

"You'll never prove that."

"Wouldn't try," Jordan said. "All I'm interested in is this bull. Take a close look."

Goddard stared at the label a moment. He shook his head, still clutching his belly. "Never seen a bull like that. Not around here."

"Somewheres else, then?"

"Nowheres else. Just never seen one."

Jordan stuffed the Bull Durham sack in his pocket. He dropped the cigarette on the floor and ground it underfoot. Then he grabbed Goddard by the shirt collar and hauled him off his knees. He slammed the livestock dealer up against the wall.

"You're startin' to make me mad. Never could abide a liar."

"I'm not lying," Goddard protested. "Honest to Christ!"

Jordan shook him so hard that the boards on the wall rattled. "You push me and I'll beat the whey out of you. Understand?"

"What the hell you want me to say? I'm tellin' you the truth."

Jordan rammed a forearm into his throat. Goddard's tongue popped out and his face suddenly turned purple. Jordan held him pinned to the wall, gasping for breath. "Wag your head when you got something to say."

Goddard nodded, and Jordan let him off the wall. He gagged, gulping in a lungful of air. Hands to his throat, he finally caught his breath. "Horse thieves don't generally run with rustlers. All I've heard are names."

"That's a start," Jordan allowed. "Who's the biggest of the lot—the top dog cow rustler."

"Fellow by the name of Bob Strickland."

"Where's he operate?"

"Down in the Nations," Goddard said. "Word has it he raids herds along the Chisholm Trail."

"What about the Texas Panhandle?"

"Got no idea, and that's the straight goods. All I know is what I've heard."

Jordan thought about it a moment. Then he abruptly turned and walked toward the door. "Appreciate your help, Mr. Goddard."

The livestock dealer looked like a man notified of a sudden reprieve. Bascom backed away, holstering his pistol as he went through the door. Outside, he joined Jordan at the hitch rack. He jerked his head at the livery stable.

"What d'you think?"

"Wasn't much," Jordan said. "But he coughed up everything he knew."

"Appears that way," Bascom agreed. " 'Course, it might be better'n it sounds. You recollect when we lost the trail at Red Deer Creek?"

Jordan looked at him. "You're thinkin' they could have trailed that bull east along the Canadian."

"Persactly," Bascom said. "And on over into the Nations."

"Maybe we ought to ride down there and have a look-see."

"What say we see the elephant first?"

Jordan laughed. "You got the urge, do you, Newt?"

"Little ring-dang-doo never hurt any man."

"Awright, pardner—let's go see the elephant."

# EIGHT

Jordan lounged back in the tub, submerged to his chin in suds. A cigarette jutted from the corner of his mouth, and he stared at the ceiling, luxuriating in the steamy hot water. He appeared lost in thought.

Earlier, after leaving the livery stable, he and Bascom had taken a room in the Dodge House. Their first priority was a bath, and they'd ordered a tub and buckets of hot water brought to the room. Bascom, like most cowhands, usually took a bath only when it rained or he forded a river. Tonight, with the prospect of women ahead, he'd felt a good scrub was in order. Still, his bath had consumed all of five minutes.

Jordan saw no need to rush the experience. He waited until Bascom's dirty water was hauled out and hot, fresh water returned. Then, lolling about in the tub, he'd scalded off an accumulation of sweat and gritty trail dust. Altogether, with the aid of a hog-bristle brush and rank yellow soap, the cleansing process had taken the better part of a half-hour. Afterward, the cigarette angled from his mouth, he surrendered himself to the steamy warmth and let his mind drift.

Upon reflection, he concluded that George Goddard was something of a disappointment. After the tip from Earp, he'd figured the livestock dealer could be persuaded to provide a solid lead. That notion had been quickly dispelled when it became apparent that Goddard dealt strictly with horse thieves. Yet any lead was better than no lead at all. Goddard had at least given them a name, and pointed them in what might prove to be the right direction. There was no doubt that the Nations swarmed with outlaws of every known variety.

With all he'd learned, however, Jordan was still stumped. Why anyone would steal a prize bull remained a mystery. But the information extracted from Goddard raised an even broader question. Why would anyone trail the stolen bull into the Nations? The Five Civilized Tribes were farmers, not ranchers. There was no ready market for a blue-blooded bull even among tame Indians. All of which added another piece to an already scrambled jigsaw puzzle. The Nations seemed an unlikely place to look for a Durham bull.

Ashes dropped off his cigarette into the soapy water. He blinked, still staring at the ceiling, struck by a wayward thought. Perhaps that was what the rustlers had intended all along. Trail the bull into the Nations, where no one would think to look, and hide it out until the dust settled. Then, after a suitable period of time, the bull could be sold with little fear of being caught. In that light, it made sense why the trail had been lost at Red Deer Creek. The rustlers figured nobody would believe they'd hightailed it into Indian Territory. And they'd figured right!

Instead of following the Canadian eastward, he and Bascom had headed north, into No Man's Land. Far from outsmarting their quarry, they had been outsmarted themselves. Which only went to prove that you should never try to second-guess a thief. The bastards seldom ever ran true to form.

"Gawddamn, Sam, you gonna lollygag around all night?"

Jordan's reverie was broken. Bascom was trimming his mustache, staring in the mirror back at the tub. He had changed into his clean set of duds and he reeked of bay rum lotion. Clearly, he was ready to howl with the ladies.

"C'mon, for chrissakes!" he said. "Haul your butt outta that tub and let's go."

"What's wrong?" Jordan goaded him. "Got an itch you can't scratch?"

"Damn right! I'm fixin' to cut the wolf loose. Wild women, that's my meat!"

Jordan doused his cigarette in the bathwater. He climbed from the tub and toweled himself dry. While Bascom urged him on, he donned fresh clothes and strapped on his gun belt. He barely had time to grab his hat before Bascom hustled him out the door.

Nightfall was descending as they crossed the railroad tracks. The South Side was wide open and running wild, the boardwalks already packed with carousing trailhands. Directly ahead lay the Lady

Gay and the Comique, the favorite watering holes of
Texas cowmen. Within easy walking distance, drunk
or sober, was a thriving infestation of gaming dens,
dance halls, and parlor houses. A rough-and-ready
form of free enterprise prevailed in the vice district.

The idea was to send the Texans back down the
trail with sore heads and empty pockets. The sporting
element had perfected it to a near science, and they
supplied all the temptation necessary. Wicked
women, pandemic games of chance, and enough popskull whiskey to ossify even the strongest man's gizzard. It was a bizarre and ribald circus, irresistible.

Jordan and Bascom pushed through the bat-wing
doors of the Comique. A band was blaring away on
the upper balcony, and shouting cowhands whirled
girls around the dance floor like a gang of acrobatic
wrestlers. The women were all fluffy curls and
heaving breasts, decked out like Kewpie dolls in
spangles and warpaint. Their shrill laughter mingled
with the raucous rebel yells of the trailhands.

The bar was lined three-deep, still another array
of girls mixed with the drinkers. The back bar was a
gaudy clutch of bottles, with a French mirror
flanked by paintings of lewd women in suggestive
poses. As Bascom elbowed a path through the
crowd, a lanky Texan, glass in hand, toppled to the
floor. Stepping across him, Bascom and Jordan
wedged into the hole. Bascom whacked the counter
with the flat of his hand.

"Barkeep! You got a couple of thirsty men here.
Start pourin' and don't stop!"

One of the bartenders hustled forward. He placed

shot glasses in front of them and produced a bottle of whiskey. With a deft touch, he filled the glasses to the brim, then corked the bottle. He tapped the counter with his knuckles.

"Dollar a shot, boys. Pay as you go."

"Dollar!" Bascom roared. "What the hell's in that bottle?"

"Best whiskey west of Kansas City."

"By God, I'd hope so—dollar a shot!"

Jordan dropped a double eagle on the counter. "Leave the bottle and call it even."

The barkeep collected the gold piece. As he walked off, his gaze shifted to a girl standing with a couple of trailhands. He flipped the coin with his thumb, plucked it out of midair, and nodded back at Jordan and Bascom. The girl glanced along the bar, then gave him a knowing wink. With a bright smile, she disengaged herself from the Texans, playfully patting them on the cheeks. She strolled off to a chorus of drunken protests.

Jordan caught the byplay out of the corner of his eye. He took a sip of whiskey, aware that the girl was drifting toward them. Bascom tossed off a shot and smacked his lips in appreciation. He poured a refill from the bottle.

The girl stopped beside Jordan. Her lips were bright crimson, eyelids shadowed with kohl, and her cheeks were tinted coral. She flashed a gleaming smile.

"Hi there, Tex! Buy a girl a drink?"

Jordan looked her up and down. She wore a skimpy peek-a-boo gown which displayed her breasts and long, lissome legs. Her hair was piled atop her head in ringlets and her eyes held a certain bawdy wisdom. She smiled, waiting until he finished his inspection.

"Do I pass muster, honeybun?"

"Yeah, real nice," Jordan said. "'Course, I'm a married man and got a passel of kids. Maybe you ought to talk to my partner."

The girl gave him an odd look. Yet she didn't miss a beat. Her bee-stung smile still fixed in place, she turned to Bascom. His mustache lifted in a wide grin.

"Howdy, ma'am," he said, leaning closer. "You're lookin' at a man with the sap runnin' high. What say we get acquainted?"

"Oooo, a sport!" Her lips curved in a teasing smile. "Well, maybe we could have ourselves a few laughs."

"Depends on where the laughs lead. I'm short on time and set to howl. Gotta hit the trail come sunrise."

She batted her lashes. "Why don't we have a drink and talk about it?"

"Sounds reasonable."

Bascom hooked the bottle off the counter. He nodded to Jordan with a broad grin. Then he walked off, his arm cinched around the girl's waist. They moved through the crowd, searching for an empty table.

Jordan watched a moment before turning back to the bar. A Texan beside him pushed a bottle along the counter. "Have a drink," he said. "Looks like your pardner's gonna be occupied awhile."

"Much obliged," Jordan said, pouring himself a refill. "How long you been in Dodge?"

"Couple of days. Name's Sim Walker, trail boss for the Rocker R. Down Sweetwater way."

Jordan introduced himself and they shook hands. "I'm from the Panhandle," he said, pulling out the makings. "Guess you must've come up the Western Trail?"

"Straight through Injun country. Had to pay off them redsticks in beeves to keep from gettin' raided."

"Comanches must've learned a trick or two from the Civilized Tribes. Over on the Chisholm they make you pay in hard cash. So much a head."

"Ain't that a fact!" Walker agreed. "Trailed a herd through the Nations last summer. Mexican bandits got nothin' on the Cherokee."

Jordan finished rolling his cigarette and struck a match. "Not just the Cherokee," he remarked, exhaling smoke. "Heard tell there's white rustlers operating along the Chisholm."

Walker knocked back a drink. "Got hit over there last summer. Lost better'n a hundred head to the bastards."

"How'd you know they were white?"

"Caught one," Walker said. "Hit us at night, but we winged one through the shoulder. Knocked him clean off his horse."

Jordan looked interested. "Turn him over to the law?"

"Hell, there ain't no law in the Nations. We hung the sorry sonovabitch."

"Say anything before you stretched his neck?"

"Spilled his guts and then some. Told us he was ridin' for some jasper name of Strickland. Didn't make no nevermind, though. We hung him anyway."

Jordan caught a reflection in the back bar mirror. He turned as Wyatt Earp halted a step away. The lawman fixed him with an icy glare. "Gave you fair warning, Jordan. What you done to George Goddard warrants an assault charge."

"Goddard's a thief," Jordan said flatly. "Why don't you arrest him?"

"Not arresting anybody. What I'm doing is posting you out of town. Be gone by sunrise."

"Guess we both lucked out, marshal. I already planned to leave, anyway."

"See that you do," Earp said. "And don't come back."

Jordan's smile was cold. "That depends on whether or not I've got business in Dodge. If I do, you won't stop me."

"No?" Earp bristled. "Try it and find out."

"Well, in the meantime, kiss Goddard goodbye for me. Tell him, no hard feelings."

Earp glowered at him a long moment. Jordan held his gaze, clearly ready to take it the next step. At last, hesitant to push further, Earp turned away. He strode toward the door.

"Jesus Pesus," Walker said in wonder. "You made the S.O.B. haul water."

"Don't kid yourself," Jordan said seriously. "Earp's got plenty of sand. Tonight just wasn't his night."

"All the same, you backed him down. Never thought I'd see it."

"Hell, forget Earp. Tell me some more about this *hombre* you hung."

Walker poured a fresh round of drinks. "What do you wanna know?"

"For openers"—Jordan took a long drag on his cigarette—"what'd he say about this Strickland? Everything you recollect."

Walker told him the story, from beginning to end.

# NINE

Their route took them southeast across Kansas. Four days out of Dodge City, they crossed the line into Indian Territory. The Chisholm Trail, thick with bawling herds of cattle, stretched endlessly southward. After skirting the trail, they followed the winding course of the Arkansas River.

Jordan and Bascom were pleasantly surprised by the Cherokee Nation. They were accustomed to treeless, windswept plains, inhospitable country. By contrast the Nations were a land of rolling hills, and farther south, certain parts were distinctly mountainous. The rainfall was also heavier than on the plains, and dense woodlands covered much of the terrain. Spongy bottomland along the river was choked with canebrakes and vast thickets of blackjack.

Also unlike the plains, the Nations were a wildlife paradise. While the buffalo herds had migrated westward, there was still an abundance of game. Great flocks of turkey swarmed over the woodlands; at dusk the timber along feeder creeks was loaded with roosting birds. Deer were plentiful,

and grouse and plover were everywhere. Fat, lazy
fish crowded the river shallows, eager to take a hook
baited with grasshopper. It was a land where no man
need go hungry.

That night they pitched camp along the riverbank. From their years spent outdoors, their routine
was well established. Jordan took care of camp
chores, and Bascom attended to hunting and cooking. After staking out their horses, Jordan began collecting wood for a fire. Bascom hefted his rifle and
walked off along a creek feeding into the river. A
short while later he returned with a plump turkey,
the head shot clean off.

By sundown a spit loaded with dressed wildfowl
was roasting to a golden brown. With the coffeepot
bubbling, there was nothing to do but wait and savor
the blend of aromas. Seated on the ground, away
from the heat of the fire, Jordan began rolling a cigarette. Bascom, who was lounging nearby, stared
silently into the flames.

Jordan lit his smoke. He took a drag, watching
Bascom a moment. "Why the faraway look?" he
asked. "Still daydreaming about your ladylove back
in Dodge?"

"That'll be the day!" Bascom grunted. "Love 'em
and leave 'em, that's my motto."

"Well, you're cogitating on something. You plan
to keep it a secret all night?"

"Nothin' secret about it. Already told you, I'm
wonderin' if we're on a wild-goose chase."

"God," Jordan said, exhaling smoke. "Your
mama raised a real worrywart, didn't she?"

"Think so, huh?" Bascom spat tobacco juice, extinguishing an ember at the edge of the fire. "Truth to tell, you ain't so consarned certain your own self."

"Tell you what I do know for certain. That blubbergut Goddard, and the trail boss I met in the Comique told the same story. The biggest he-wolf rustler in these parts is named Bob Strickland."

"For all we know that trail boss could've been spinnin' a windy. No way to prove he hung anybody, much less one of Strickland's gang."

Jordan flicked an ash off his cigarette. "How else would he have got Strickland's name?"

"Beats me," Bascom said idly. "I wasn't there to hear his story."

"Bet your boots you weren't! You were off gettin' your dauber dipped with that soiled dove."

"You sound just a touch jealous. Oughta got your own pole greased while you had the chance."

Jordan smiled. "Quit changing the subject on me. What's troubling you?"

A moment passed. Then, motioning off into the distance, Bascom frowned. "Guess crossin' the line got me a little spooked. Down here, anybody on the level's liable to get his gizzard cooked."

Bascom's statement underscored a critical problem. Law enforcement in the Nations was a grueling business, conducted under the strangest circumstances ever faced by men who wore badges. With the advancement of frontier settlements, a new pattern of lawlessness began to emerge on the plains. The era of the lone bandit gradually evolved into something far worse. Outlaws began to run in packs.

Local peace officers found themselves unable to cope with the vast distances involved. Gangs made lightning strikes in Kansas and Missouri, terrorizing the settlements, then retreated into the Nations. These wild forays, particularly bank holdups and train robberies, were executed with daring and precision. Limited by state jurisdiction, local lawmen could not cross the territorial line. So the war soon became a grisly contest between gangs and the federal marshals. But it was hide-and-seek with a unique advantage falling to the outlaws.

Once in the Nations the gangs found virtual immunity from the law. By any yardstick, they enjoyed the oddest sanctuary in the history of crime. The Five Civilized Tribes were comprised of the Cherokee, Creek, Choctaw, Chickasaw and Seminole. While each tribe maintained Light Horse Police, their authority extended only to Indian citizens. However terrible the offense, white men were exempt from all prosecution except that of a federal court. It was the U.S. Marshals who had to pursue and capture every white outlaw. The Nations had quickly become infested with fugitives from justice.

The problem was compounded by the Indians themselves. All too often the red men connived with the outlaws, offering them asylum. Few in the Nations had any respect for white man's law, and the marshals were looked upon as intruders. So the job of ferreting out and capturing lawbreakers became a herculean task. To add yet another obstacle, even the terrain favored the outlaws. A man could lose himself in the mountains or along wooded river bottoms and live outdoors for extended periods of time in relative comfort. Tracking badmen into the Nations was a dirty, dangerous business. No job for the faint of heart.

The small number of federal marshals gave the outlaws a deadly edge. The favorable terrain and a general atmosphere of sanctuary were further improved by too few lawmen chasing too many desperadoes. The Nations swarmed with killers and robbers and dozens of gangs like the one led by Bob Stickland. Outnumbered and outgunned, marshals were forced to ride alone into Indian Territory. Any lawman who crossed the line was constantly faced with the specter of his own death.

"Lawdogs have it bad," Bascom said now. "You and me are a heap worse off. We got no tin star."

Jordan shrugged. "A marshal's not able to hide behind his badge. Fact is, it might get him killed quicker."

"I reckon that's my point. Without a badge, we're liable to get killed double-quick."

"Hell, Newt, we've been on our lonesome anytime we took the trail. You'll recollect we've been shot at before."

"The Nations are different," Bascom countered. "Anyplace else, law-abiding folks are leastways neutral. Down here, that ain't the case."

Jordan studied the coal on the tip of his cigarette. "You're saying we might have trouble with the Indians too—that it?"

"'Specially if they figger out who we are. They'd peg us no better'n bounty hunters."

"And white bounty hunters, at that."

"Natural fact," Bascom said, nodding. "These people got no love for anybody white. Heard tell they call us *tibos*, and that ain't no compliment."

Jordan agreed that the Nations were another world entirely. The root of the problem was that so many whites coveted Indian lands. The Cherokee Outlet, one of the federal government's more bizarre creations, was a particularly sore point. Earlier in the century, when the Cherokee were resettled in Indian Territory, they were granted seven million acres bordering southern Kansas. At the same time they were also granted a westward corridor, providing a gateway to the distant buffalo ranges. Comprising more than six million acres, roughly 150 miles in length, it was designated the Cherokee Outlet. The legal status of this strip was confounding from the start.

Though the Cherokee held title to the Outlet, they were forbidden to dispose of it in any manner. Their lands to the east were adequate for the entire tribe, and as a result they seldom ventured into their western grant. The upshot was a huge land mass that had remained unoccupied for the past thirty years. All that changed, however, when the Chisholm Trail was blazed through Indian Territory. Texas cattlemen discovered a lush stretch of graze watered by the Canadian and Cimarron Rivers. The Outlet made a perfect holding ground for longhorns, where cows were fattened out before the final drive to railhead.

Word of the grassy paradise quickly drew the attention of white homesteaders. In short order, a public outcry arose over settlement of the Cherokee Outlet. The settlers were backed by the railroads and merchant princes, all of whom had a vested interest in the westward expansion. Alone in their opposition to settlement were the Five Civilized Tribes, led by the Cherokee. Their dealings with the government over several generations had formed a chain of broken pledges and unfulfilled treaties. They saw settlement as a device for the enrichment of white farmers and greedy politicians.

In Washington, those same politicians were holding out a wide array of enticements. Efforts were underway to bribe the Cherokee into allowing settlement of the Outlet. At the same time a campaign was organized to convince the Five Civilized Tribes that their best interests would be served by abolishing tribal government. They were told that full citizenship within the Republic would afford them equality before the law, voting rights, and improved schooling. In return, all they had to do was to surrender their lands to settlement.

Based on their experience with *tibos*' promises, the Five Civilized Tribes had good reason to doubt the faith of the government. However strong the arguments, they were unwilling to exchange independence for the dubious privilege of citizenship. Indian leaders, as well as the lowliest tribesmen, preferred the old ways to the white man's road. Yet the assault from Washington was unrelenting, and the Cherokee were at the forefront of the fight. Over the last few years they had grown increasingly hostile toward *tibos*, particularly strangers. Apart from outlaws, no white man was welcome in the Cherokee Nation.

"Guess you're right," Jordan said at length. "We'd better hatch ourselves a damn good story. Some reason for being here."

Bascom moved to the bed of glowing embers. He rotated the turkey on the spit, then settled back on his haunches. "Any idjit would spot our saddle gear for Texan. We'd best stick close to home."

"Wouldn't hurt to have something in common with this Strickland. Why not pass ourselves off as rustlers?"

"Not a bad idea. We could say we got identified and outrun the law. Figgered to hole up in the Nations a spell."

Jordan considered, puffing on his cigarette. "Where'd all this happen? Has to be someplace besides the Panhandle."

"How about west of Fort Worth, out on the Brazos? Not likely we'd stumble across anybody from there."

"We know all the brands out that way. So nobody could trip us up with questions."

"That's a fact," Bascom agreed. "Tell 'em we're on the dodge and lookin' to hook up with an outfit. Got tired of workin' penny-ante deals on our own."

"Has a good ring to it," Jordan said. "Just ordinary enough to be true."

"Hope it works with any Injuns we run across. I wouldn't want to get scalped."

"C'mon, Newt, the Cherokees don't take hair anymore. They're part of the Civilized Tribes."

"Says you," Bascom muttered. "I'll believe it when I see it."

After supper, they bedded down for the night. Stuffed with roast turkey, Jordan stared thoughtfully at the starry sky. He wondered whether it was true, whether the Cherokee really were civilized. True or not, they were about to find out.

# TEN

Tahlequah was the capital of the Cherokee Nation. Set among gently rolling hills, it lay some eighty miles south of the Kansas border. To many, it was considered the hub of progress in Indian Territory.

Jordan and Bascom had ridden into town from the west. After six days on the trail, they looked the part of men who slept under the stars. They had decided that their search for Bob Strickland should begin in Tahlequah. As the largest town in the Cherokee Nation, it seemed the logical place to start.

Neither of them appeared weary from their journey. Quite the contrary, their expressions were wide-eyed with wonder, somewhat awestruck. Nothing they'd heard about the Five Civilized Tribes had prepared them for what they had seen that morning. The Cherokee, in particular, were more civilized than anything they might have imagined.

For the last few hours they had passed magnificent baronial homes, with colonnaded porches an-

chored by towering Grecian columns. The setting
was one of antebellum plantations transplanted
from a more gracious era. The lavish estates were
outnumbered by log cabins and unpretentious frame
houses; yet it was obvious that wealthy Cherokee
lived on a scale befitting their position. Before reset-
tlement to Indian Territory, the Cherokee's ancestral
lands had been located in the Old South. Clearly, a
holdover from that distant culture had stayed with
them on the trip westward.

Bascom, more so than Jordan, was dumbstruck.
The extent of the Cherokee's progress along the
white man's road left him confused, hardly able to
credit his eyes. He expected to find advanced sav-
ages, a step above the nomadic Plains Tribes. At
most, he thought to encounter redskins who had
evolved into tillers of the soil after being pacified by
the federal government. Instead he found a people
who cultivated the land with something approaching
reverence. Theirs was a thriving agrarian society that
rivaled even the most prosperous farm community in
Texas.

Tahlequah itself proved to be yet another marvel.
Directly ahead, across the town square, was the
capitol building. A large, two-story brick structure,
it was fronted by a sweeping portico only slightly
less stately than the one in Austin, the Texas capital.
There was an air of bustling efficiency about the
place, and to Bascom's amazement, a group of men
gathered on the capitol steps were dressed in swal-
lowtail coats and top hats. In contrast, his own
clothes were caked with sweat and grime, and

bearded stubble covered his jaw. The term "Civilized Tribes" suddenly took on new meaning.

The town square was spacious and well kept, dominated by a sturdy brick hotel and several business establishments. Jordan, no less than Bascom, was stunned to see a newspaper office, with a hand-lettered sign for the *Cherokee Advocate* on the plate glass window. They dismounted outside a mercantile and stood for a moment, scanning the square. On the boardwalks, the sight of Cherokee women in white women's dresses merely added to their sense of bemusement. They exchanged a look, shaking their heads, as they entered the store.

Behind the counter, a clerk with black hair and pale reddish skin watched them approach. His eyes were not friendly. "Help you?"

"Sure hope so," Jordan said. "I'm about out of smokin' tobacco. Don't suppose you'd stock Bull Durham?"

The clerk looked offended. He gestured to a display case somewhat farther down the counter. There, on the glass front, was a painted replica of the Bull Durham label, complete with the bull. Jordan stared at it with an odd expression.

"How much you want?" the clerk asked.

"I'll take ten bags."

The clerk placed them on the counter. "Anything else?"

"Guess you've got Arbuckle's coffee, too?"

"How much?"

"A pound will do it."

The clerk moved to a large galvanized container

and removed a scoop. He bagged the coffee beans, then placed the bag on a scale. Satisfied, he folded the top of the bag and set it on the counter.

"Coffee and tobacco," he said. "One dollar even."

Jordan dropped a silver dollar on the counter. "Where's the nearest blacksmith?"

"Straight across the square and down the street."

Outside the store, Bascom wagged his head. "Unfriendly cuss, wasn't he?"

"Like you said, Newt, we're *tibos*."

"Guess the shoe's on the other foot."

"Come again?"

"Well, a Cherokee wouldn't get no better treatment down in Texas. They're just feedin' us a dose of our own medicine."

Jordan couldn't argue the point. After stowing the goods, they mounted and reined away from the store. As they rode across the square, a group of men on the capitol building steps fell silent, watching them closely. They were all too aware of the scrutiny, the cold stares.

A small sign over the smithy door identified the proprietor as Benjamin Tappin. When they entered, Tappin turned from the forge, his shirt soaked with sweat. He was stoutly built, with dark skin, as though he'd been dipped in a tanning vat. He nodded pleasantly.

"Morning."

"Howdy," Jordan said. "Got time to have a look at our horses?"

"All the time in the world, friend."

The blacksmith's tone surprised them. He

smiled, moving outside, and walked to their mounts. With a gentle voice, calming the horses, he inspected their shoes hoof by hoof. Finished, he turned back to where Jordan and Bascom stood in the wide doorway.

"Looks fine," Tappin observed. "What made you think anything was wrong?"

In the course of their work, Jordan and Bascom had become accomplished liars. An undercover assignment required duplicity, and they played their roles with some skill. Jordan spread his hands in a casual gesture.

"Never know when you'll run across a smith. Figured we ought to have things checked out."

"All I did was look, so there's no charge."

"Well, thank you kindly, Mr. Tappin. You the only smith hereabouts?"

"Only one in Tahlequah," Tappin replied. "What makes you ask?"

"We're just up from Texas," Jordan told him. "Lookin' for a friend of ours, name of Bob Strickland. Thought you might know him."

"Why would I know him?"

"Bob's mighty particular about his horse. Has the critter shod pretty regular."

"Sorry," Tappin said mildly. "Don't know anyone by that name."

"Figured it was a long shot. Never hurts to ask, though."

"Look here," Bascom interjected. "Wonder if you'd satisfy my curiosity about something?"

"If I can," Tappin said. "What's the question?"

"Well, like Sam told you, we're strangers in these parts. We're sorta curious about the town and all them gents in fancy duds. Wasn't exactly what we expected, know what I mean?"

"Sure do," Tappin said amiably. "Most white folks don't know what to make of the Cherokee."

Bascom grinned. "By golly, you hit the nail right on the head! How's things work around here, anyway?"

Tappin proved to be a garrulous talker. He was proud of his heritage, clearly open to educating a couple of *tibos*. The Cherokee Nation, he explained, was an independent republic. For practical reasons the Cherokee's form of government was patterned on that of the white man. A tribal chief acted as the head of state, and the tribal council, similar in structure to Congress, was comprised of two houses. All government offices, as well as the council chambers, were housed in the capitol building.

Of all Indian tribes, Tappin went on to relate, the Cherokee was the only one with an alphabet. Their language could therefore be written, books and newspapers printed. In 1851, the tribal leaders had established elementary schools, as well as a system of higher education. Seminaries, one for boys and another for girls, were constructed some five miles south of Tahlequah. Among other subjects, the children were taught Latin and algebra, grammar and science. While their schooling was conducted in English, they were also grounded in their tribal language. The most promising students were later sent to colleges and universities back East. In effect, the Cherokee Nation was looking to the future by preparing their children to deal with the white man's world. The best of each generation were trained in business and law and medicine.

"Other tribes," Tappin concluded proudly, "aren't like the Cherokee. We go about things in a real modern way."

Bascom chuckled, clearly astounded. "Wish't I'd been raised here. Hell, I never got past my three R's."

Before Tappin could reply, a uniformed Cherokee approached the blacksmith shop. He was solidly built, with a hawklike nose and high cheekbones. His badge, and the stripes on his jacket, identified him as a sergeant in the Light Horse Police.

"Afternoon," he said, nodding to Jordan and Bascom. "You men have business in Tahlequah?"

"None to speak of," Jordan said casually. "Just passing through."

"Understood you bought tobacco and coffee over at the store. Not much supplies for men on the road."

Strange white men were suspect anywhere in the Nations. The sergeant's remark indicated that the store clerk had alerted the Light Horse Police. The remark also had an immediate effect on Tappin's attitude. Friendly a moment before, he now cut a suspicious, sideways glance at Jordan and Bascom.

"Something more to it," he said, addressing the sergeant. "Told me they're just up from Texas. Asked if I know a man named Bob Strickland."

The uniformed Cherokee gave them a hard-eyed look. "I'm Sergeant Elias Reed, Light Horse Police. You'd best give me a straight answer. Are you men U.S. Marshals?"

Bascom woofed laughter. "Gawddamn, that plumb beats all! Nobody ever before accused us of being lawdogs."

"So who are you?" Reed demanded. "Why are you asking about Bob Strickland?"

Jordan pulled out the makings. "Look here, sergeant," he said, spilling tobacco into the paper, "we had a little trouble down in Texas. Figured we'd try our luck in the Nations."

"What kind of trouble?"

"Nothing serious." Jordan popped a match, lit his cigarette. "Honest dispute over who owned some cows."

Sergeant Reed stared at him. "You talking about rustled cows?"

"No sirree!" Bascom protested. "Feller got us mixed up with somebody else. We're clean as a whistle!"

"Your business below the Red River doesn't interest me. What does interest me is why you're looking for Strickland."

Jordan took a chance. "Somebody told us Strickland's on good terms with the Cherokee. Just thought we'd hook up with him, that's all."

Reed studied them a moment. His mouth lifted in a slight smile. "In plain language, you're looking for a place to hide out—aren't you?"

"Well—" Jordan offered an abashed shrug. "I reckon we wouldn't mind stickin' around. Always heard the Cherokee are hospitable people."

"You cause any trouble and I'll personally turn you over to the federal marshals. Understood?"

"We're the peaceable sort," Bascom assured him. "Don't worry yourself on that score."

"Your worry, not mine." Reed hesitated, then abruptly nodded. "Head northwest, forty miles or so up the Verdigris River. You'll find a trading post, owned by Will Musgrave."

"This Musgrave," Jordan inquired, "he a friend of Strickland's?"

"Ask him and find out."

"Maybe he won't cotton to a couple of strangers."

"Tell him Elias Reed sent you."

"I'm obliged, sergeant. That's damned square of you."

Reed smiled. "Welcome to the Cherokee Nation."

# ELEVEN

**H**ow do we play it?"

"Stick to our story," Jordan said. "Worked good enough in Tahlequah. No reason it won't work here."

Bascom thought about it. "Strickland's liable to be a mite more suspicious than that Cherokee Light Horse."

"Wouldn't surprise me a bit. We'll just have to convince him we're true-blue desperadoes."

"What if he don't have the bull no more? Hell, for that matter, what if he's not the one that stole the bull?"

"Quit borrowin' trouble," Jordan advised. "We've got to follow our best hunch. Strickland's the pick of the litter just now."

"Yeah, I suppose," Bascom conceded. " 'Course, I'm still not so all-fired certain about that Light Horse feller. Could be a trap of some sort."

"C'mon, Newt! Reed bought our story hook, line and sinker. What kind of trap you talking about?"

Bascom leaned sideways in his saddle. He splat-

tered a tree at trailside with tobacco juice, then
wiped his mustache. "Just suppose this place we're
headed is a deadfall. Maybe the people they send up
here don't never come back."

"You got a powerful imagination," Jordan said.
"You think this Musgrave—the one that owns the
place—kills off anybody Reed sends his way. Is
that it?"

"Who knows?" Bascom seemed perplexed.
"Damn good way to get rid of folks that appear a
touch too nosy. We'd be dead and buried, and
who's to know the difference? Nobody in the Nations would come askin' questions."

"Like I said before, you worry too much."

"Nothin' wrong with a man being careful. Beats
the bejesus out of gettin' yourself killed."

Jordan chuckled. "In for a dime, in for a dollar,
Newt. We'll just have to play the hand out."

"You always was a gawddamn daredevil. Wonder
you haven't got me murdered before now."

"Well, like they say, nobody lives forever."

"Jesus!"

Late yesterday they had departed Tahlequah.
Their route had taken them through a land heavily
forested and largely unsettled. The few farms they'd
come across were modest plots hacked from rough
terrain, or located in sparsely wooded valleys. They
had camped for the night along the lower reaches of
the Verdigris River, some miles northwest of the
Cherokee capitol. That morning, they had broken
camp as dawn lighted the horizon.

A crude winding trail bordered the river. On either side of the river the countryside swept away in broken hills and timbered wilderness. There was a foreboding sense about the landscape, as though it had been frozen in time and forgotten. Tangled underbrush and still shadows in the woods merely added to the forlorn, somewhat ominous, feel of their surroundings. All day, riding mostly in silence, they had seen no one on the trail.

Dusk settled on the land as they rounded a sharp bend in the river. Ahead lay a large natural clearing, bordered by woods and stretching for some fifty yards along the shoreline. On a slight rise, set well back away from the river, stood a crude log structure flanked by a corral. There were several horses in the corral, and a tendril of smoke drifted from a stovepipe jutting through the roof. From the distance they'd travelled, they knew they had stumbled upon Will Musgrave's trading post.

The remote setting was by design, purposely planned. Federal law prohibited the sale of spirits, whether beer or whiskey, anywhere within the borders of Indian Territory. Violation of the law was punishable by a stiff fine, often accompanied by a term of two or three years in federal prison. The prohibition was enforced by U.S. Marshals, who were preoccupied for the most part with tracking bank robbers and killers. Yet the marshals were always on the scout for whiskey runners, or illegal stills. The backwoods location of the trading post was in itself a deterrent to lawmen. Any man wearing a star was fair game in wilderness regions of the Nations.

Jordan and Bascom dismounted outside the corral. They left their horses tied to the crossbars and
walked toward the front of the trading post. The
building was large and solidly constructed, with one
window set into the wall on the far side of the door.
When they entered, they were greeted by the ripe
odor of wood smoke, animal hides and whiskey. The
interior was dim and shadowed, lighted only by
coal-oil lamps and darkening twilight from the window. They halted just inside the door, their eyes ad-
justing to the dusky light.

A long counter occupied the far side of the room.
One end was devoted to liquor and the other to
trade. The back wall was lined with shelves, trade
goods randomly displayed for barter or purchase. To
the left, boxes of assorted supplies were stacked
amidst piles of deer hides and furry pelts. To the
right were tables and chairs, situated near a huge
potbellied stove. Doors on either side of the room
gave off onto the kitchen and a passageway lined
with sleeping quarters.

Three men were scattered about the room. One
stood behind the counter, clearly a mixed-blood
Cherokee. A white man, dressed in range clothes,
leaned against the counter holding a whiskey glass.
Another white man, somewhat more finely attired,
sat at one of the tables shuffling a deck of cards.
Their expressions were neutral, assessing the two
strangers in the doorway. Finally, the man behind
the counter motioned them forward.

"C'mon in," he said in a jocular voice. "You
gents lost, are you?"

"Not just exactly," Jordan said. "Leastways, we're at the right place if your name's Will Musgrave."

A young girl, quite pretty, with dark raven hair, appeared in the door leading to the kitchen. Jordan glanced at her as he and Bascom walked toward the counter. Her complexion indicated that she, too, was of Cherokee blood. Musgrave smiled good-naturedly as they halted before the counter.

"You found the place and the man. How'd you come to know my name?"

"Elias Reed," Jordan said. "Sergeant with the Light Horse. He told us to ask for you personal."

"You must've hit it off with Elias. He generally sends white men packin' for parts unknown."

Bascom chortled softly. "There at first, that's exactly what happened. Told us to light a shuck *muy pronto.*"

Musgrave looked interested. "What changed his mind?"

"Well, sir—" Bascom edged closer, lowered his voice. "You might say we wore out our welcome down below the Red. Some folks ain't got no sense of humor."

"Lemme guess," Musgrave said, grinning. "You're on the dodge, and you're lookin' for a hidey-hole. Elias wouldn't've sent you here otherwise. Am I close?"

"Red-hot," Bascom admitted. "Got in a dispute with some jasper over who owned a bunch of cows."

"Lots of people I know have the same problem. Tell me, though, why didn't you just stop north of the Red? Why'd you come all the way to Cherokee land?"

Jordan spread his hands. "We're trying to hook up with a friend of a friend. Reed told us he's a regular customer of yours."

"What's his name . . . this friend of a friend?"

"Bob Strickland."

Musgrave's smile slipped. His expression turned somber. "Hate to break the news," he said, "but you fellows rode a long way for nothin'. Day before yesterday, Bob Strickland got hisself killed."

Jordan and Bascom required no pretense. Their faces were etched with astonishment. Jordan was first to recover himself.

"How'd it happen?"

"Guess Bob's luck finally run out. Federal marshals jumped him and his boys, and all hell busted loose. When the smoke cleared, Bob was deader'n cooked meat."

"Damn," Jordan said tightly. "We figured to join up with his bunch. Anybody get away?"

"Way I hear it," Musgrave related, "them that was left scattered to the wind. Likely took off for the Choctaw Nation. Things are quieter down there."

"Helluva note," Bascom muttered darkly. "We sorta had our hopes pinned on Strickland."

"What's you gents' names, anyway?"

"I'm Newt Bascom and this here's Sam Jordan. You might've already guessed we're Texicans. Not that it meants a hill of beans now."

Bascom's dispirited tone was genuine. He and Jordan had staked everything on Strickland being their man. But now, with the news of Strickland's death, they were confronted with a complete washout. For all practical purposes, they were back where they'd started.

"Sounds like a crock of shit to me."

The man at the end of the counter turned to face them. He was burly, heavily muscled, with a wild thatch of hair spilling from beneath his hat. He stared at them with a sour look.

"I'm takin' bets you assholes are Texas Rangers, or some such. Up here on the scout for ol' Bob."

Jordan reacted quickly to squelch the thought. He shoved away from the counter, advancing on the man. "Newt and me don't take kindly to insults. Before I get there, you'd better start eatin' crow."

The man grabbed for a holstered pistol on his hip. Jordan was a shade faster, closing the distance before he cleared leather. One foot planted, Jordan lashed out with the other and his bootheel thudded into the man's kneecap. There was a muted crack, and the man screamed, doubling at the waist.

Jordan straightened him upright with a sizzling uppercut. Then, like bolts of lightning, he delivered a sharp left hook and crossed with a hammering right to the jaw. The man went down as though he'd been shot with an elephant gun. Hardly hesitating, Jordan grabbed him by the collar and dragged him across the floor. Opening the door, he hefted the man upright and dumped him outside. After he slammed the door, he turned back into the room, dusting his hands off.

"Never could stand a dim-dot with a big mouth."

"Bravo! Good riddance to bad rubbish."

Everyone turned to the man seated at the table. He

wore a black suit, with white shirt and string tie, and a black flatcrowned hat. His dark hair was set off by a neatly groomed mustache, and his hands were those of a man unaccustomed to hard labor. His trade, to anyone familiar with gaming dens, was that of professional gambler.

"Mr. Jordan," he said with a dashing grin. "I do admire neat work. Would you and Mr. Bascom join me for a drink?"

Bascom followed Jordan across the room. At the table, they saw that a portable faro layout was arranged before the gambler. He rose from his chair and shook their hands.

"Earl McCord," he said genially. "Games of chance are my trade. Won't you have a seat?"

Musgrave brought a bottle and glasses as they seated themselves. Jordan rolled a cigarette while the drinks were poured. Watching the gambling man, it occurred to him that they might have played into luck. McCord lifted his glass in a toast.

"Very handily done, Mr. Jordan. Congratulations."

"Thanks." Jordan took a sip, then lit his cigarette. "Who was that jaybird, anyhow?"

"A common ruffian." McCord's hand lifted in a dismissive gesture. "He roundly deserved the thrashing."

"I take it you're a regular around here?"

"You might say I have the gaming concession. The establishment's clientele are rolling in what might be termed ill-gotten gains."

"Like the sound of that," Jordan said. "We could use some *dinero* ourselves."

McCord laughed. "Well, gentlemen, you have indeed come to the right place."

Jordan was of the same opinion. He thought Earl McCord would prove to be a gold mine of information.

# TWELVE

**T**ime weighed heavily. Three days had passed since Jordan and Bascom rode into the trading post. No new leads had been uncovered, and their investigation appeared to be at a dead end. Lord Ingram's Durham bull now took on all the aspects of the Holy Grail. Their search had become a quest with no foreseeable resolution.

A dozen or so outlaws had wandered into the trading post over the last three days. Some were rustlers and horse thieves, and others specialized in robbing banks and trains. As a group, they were a rough lot, with no sense of camaraderie among them. Will Musgrave went out of his way to make introductions and relieve the tension caused by the presence of Jordan and Bascom. Yet the outlaws were suspicious by nature, slow to accept strangers. For the most part, they kept to themselves.

Jordan had nonetheless earned a measure of respect. The man he'd whipped, Frank Bohannon, was a loner, and a brawler of some repute. Musgrave took ill-disguised delight in relating how Jordan had cleaned his clock with no lost motion. At the end of each telling, Bascom, who was acting the role of buffoon and jester, quickly added that his partner had gone through Bohannon "like shit through a tin horn." All of which amused the assorted badmen, and caused them to treat Jordan with some deference. But they still held their distance.

The trading post had four lodging rooms. Musgrave and his daughter Hannah were quartered in two of the rooms, and Earl McCord occupied a third. Jordan and Bascom, at a charge of five dollars a night, shared the fourth room. The charge included three meals a day, and grain for their horses. The daughter's cooking was first rate, with generous portions, and Bascom remarked more than once that they were "living high on the hog." Yet the good food and clean quarters provided small respite from the overriding concern. Their investigation was stymied.

Jordan and Bascom whiled away the time at Earl McCord's faro layout. By now on a first name basis, they found him to be a genial roué with a dry, sardonic wit. His manner of speech, and a general air of refinement, indicated that he was a man of considerable education. As well, he had a gift for storytelling, and a seemingly inexhaustible supply of amusing anecdotes. All of which was part and parcel of his bag of tricks. Though he was a genius with cards, inordinately adept, Jordan and Bascom nonetheless tagged him as a skilled cardsharp. His entertaining patter was merely a device to distract those he fleeced.

After talking it over, the detectives decided to limit their losses by playing for low stakes. There was nothing to be gained by exposing him, for he was generally liked by the customers, and quite probably shared his winnings with Musgrave. A still better reason was that he proved to be a lode of information. When the three of them were alone, he had no qualms about speaking of the outlaws who dropped by the trading post. Jordan and Bascom listened, rarely prompting him with a question, for he amused himself with his caustic remarks. By the third day they'd learned everything there was to know about everyone who had entered the establishment. The disturbing part was that none of it was worth knowing. So far, the men they'd met were small-timers, not a suspect in the bunch. They bided their time, hoping for a break, and relieved the boredom at McCord's crooked table.

Faro was one of the most popular games in Western saloons and gaming dives. Its name derived from the image of an Egyptian pharaoh on the back of the cards, and the game itself had originated a century earlier in France. Once the game of choice for kings and royalty, it was now an addictive pastime for cowhands and gamblers throughout the West.

Cards were dealt from a specially adapted box, and the players bet against the dealer. Every card from ace to king was painted on the cloth layout that covered the table. A player placed his money on the card of his choice, and two cards were then drawn faceup from the box. The first card drawn lost and the second card won. The player could "copper" his play by betting a card to lose instead of win. There were twenty-five turns, since the first and last cards in the deck paid nothing. When the box was empty, the dealer shuffled and the game began anew.

McCord deftly shuffled the cards and allowed Jordan to cut. Then he placed the deck in the dealing box and burned the top card, commonly referred to as the "soda" card. Glancing up, he nodded, indicating the game was open to play. Jordan and Bascom, pretending near-poverty, were betting a quarter a hand. Bascom placed a marker above the ace, another between the five-six, and still another between the jack-queen. By playing several cards at once, he readily identified himself as an experienced gambler. The system was known as "coppering the heel," and increased the odds of winning. Jordan bet a single marker above the queen.

McCord pulled two cards from the box, a king and a four. "Almost got yourselves a winner," he said in the slick cadence of a pitchman. He scooped their markers onto his side of the table. "Get a hunch, bet a bunch."

Jordan and Bascom stuck with quarter bets. McCord was adroit and quick on the deal. His hands flashed between the box and the layout with practiced expertise. Cards popped out of the box in speedy pairs, and just as rapidly he paid the winners and collected the losers. What the detectives knew, but kept to themselves, was that he was dealing "seconds." The edge of the cards were shaved with a razor, undetectable to anyone except the knowledgeable cheat. McCord's sensitive fingers allowed him to feel the value of a particular card, and in an instant play it to his benefit. A card that gave him a loser was held back, and another card, sometimes from the bottom of the deck, was dealt instead. Any card of no consequence was spun onto the layout.

Bascom had to admire his technique. He'd played against master faro dealers—it was known as "bucking the tiger"—from Matamoros to the Kansas cow towns. But only once or twice had he butted heads with a cardsharp as slick as McCord. Not one player in a thousand would have caught anything underhanded in the swift movement of the cards. The gambler's style was all the more admirable since he foxed the suckers rather than getting greedy. He permitted the players to win occasionally, but more times than not, they walked away losers. He had a corner on the market at the trading post, and though the game was rigged, he never pressed so hard as to endanger a good thing. Bascom figured he probably pulled down close to five hundred a week.

At the end of the deal, the "hoc" card, the last card in the deck, was dropped on the table. McCord paused to light a thin, black cheroot. He offered his cigar case around, but both the detectives declined. Jordan rolled himself a cigarette and struck a match. McCord puffed thick blue smoke, then held the cheroot out for inspection.

"Fine smoke," he said, with obvious appreciation. "Discovered these in the course of my days on the old riverboats. You should try one sometime."

Jordan held out his cigarette for inspection. "While back, we got the straight goods on Bull

Durham smokin' tobacco. Know why they call it
The Genuine Article?"

"I can't say as I do."

"Anywhere you go Bull Durham is known as The
Standard of the World. Specially cured from what's
called Bright yellow-leaf tobacco."

"Interesting," McCord said. "I wasn't aware Bull
Durham had such an illustrious record."

Jordan smiled, took a deep drag. He exhaled with
great satisfaction. "Best damn smoke in all of cre-
ation. You ought to try one sometime."

McCord laughed, aware his statement on che-
roots had been turned back on him. "Touché," he
said amiably. "Perhaps I will try one."

"I'll even teach you how to roll 'em. Spoil you off
those cigars real quick."

"Certainly worth a try," McCord said, shuffling
the cards. "The board is open, gentlemen. Place your
wagers."

Jordan pushed back his chair. "Think I'll stretch
my legs. A saddle sure beats the hell out of a hard-
wood chair."

"Just got my seat warm," Bascom said with a
whiskery grin. "Feel a change of luck comin' on.
Got a hunch the worm's turned."

"That's the spirit," McCord said, smiling. "Lady
luck smiles on those who stay the course."

Jordan left them to the card game. He moved to
the door, stepping outside, and paused to survey the
countryside. The river gurgled along the shallows
and somewhere in the distance a sentry crow
sounded its warning call. There was a peaceful set-

ting to the scene that belied the conduct of business at the trading post. While Indians from the surrounding area came there to trade furs and pelts, it existed principally as a hangout for white men. A place where thieves and murderers could let off steam. Whiskey and Earl McCord's faro game were the lure.

After a last drag on his cigarette, Jordan ground it underfoot. He walked off toward the corral, thinking to have a look at the horses. As he rounded the corner of the building, he ran into Hannah Musgrave. She was returning from the henhouse out back, a basket of eggs hooked over her arm. Her dusky features flushed, and she gave him a shy smile.

"Robbin' the henhouse, are you, Miss Hannah?"

"Yes," she said, holding his gaze. "Women's chores are never done."

Jordan was all too aware of her sweet musky scent. On occasion, he'd caught her watching him, and he suspected there was invitation in her look. She was attractive, with a fetching smile and dark eyes, and her dress did nothing to conceal the ripe curves of a buxom young woman. He thought she was likely a wildcat in bed.

Thus far, their conversation had been of an impersonal nature. Last night, prompted by her father, she had related the origins of their people. In old tribal language, she'd noted, the word for Cherokee was *Tsalagi*. The ancient emblem of bravery was the color red, and bravery was believed to originate from where the sun rose. So the word *Tsalagi*, roughly translated, meant "Red Fire Men," brave men. Though the Cherokee had been transplanted from their ancestral homeland, and most had converted to the Christian faith, tribal lore had not disappeared from their lives. Even today, she'd concluded, the people still thought of themselves as the *Tsalagi*.

All the while she'd talked, she had held his gaze, ignoring Bascom. Watching her now, he was reminded that the investigation had hit a stone wall. He decided to play on the invitation in her eyes.

"Enjoyed your story last night," he said. "Too bad we won't be around to hear more about the Cherokee."

"You're leaving?" she said, suddenly alarmed. "Why?"

"Well, we can't seem to hook up with anybody around here. And McCord's just about busted us flat. Time to move on."

"Does it have to be a rustler's outfit? Couldn't you do something else?"

"Miss Hannah, cows are all I know. Trains and banks just aren't my speed. Probably get myself killed, the first robbery I pulled."

She averted her eyes. At last, as though wrestling with some inner turmoil, she looked back at him. "Dad and Earl are afraid to talk too much. They know you're perfect for somebody . . . a certain gang."

"I don't get it," Jordan said. "What are they scared of?"

"A man, the biggest rustler in the Nations. They know he'd kill them if they spilled his name."

"Does he come around here?"

"Now and then," she said. "They're waiting for him to show up, so's they can introduce you. Even then, they're not sure he'd take you on. He's awful spooky."

Jordan looked hopeful. "Anything's worth a try. What's his name?"

She hesitated a moment. "You didn't hear it from me—promise?"

"You got my solemn word, Miss Hannah."

"His name's Rafe Dolan, and you be careful. He's mean as a snake."

She hurried off, as though fearful of having spoken the name. Jordan stood there, watching her rush into the trading post. Then, silently, he repeated the name to himself. Rafe Dolan.

# THIRTEEN

After the noon meal, Jordan gave Bascom the nod. They complimented Hannah on her cooking, then left Musgrave and McCord lingering over a final cup of coffee. The girl glanced at them sharply as they went out the door.

Jordan led the way to the corral. He leaned back against the railings, and built himself a smoke. One eye on the door, he waited to make sure they wouldn't be followed. The silence finally became too much for Bascom. He sensed something was afoot.

"What's wrong? We hidin' from somebody?"

"After a fashion," Jordan said. "Wanted to make sure we could talk in private."

"Yeah?" Bascom said, his interest piqued. "What about?"

"Musgrave and McCord have been holding out. Seems like there's a hotshot rustler hereabouts. Way I heard it, he's the biggest in the Nations."

"Tarnation! Ain't you the one? You got the girl to talk, didn't you?"

"More or less." Jordan inhaled, savored the smoke. "She didn't tell me a whole helluva lot. But it's a lead—of sorts."

"So?" Bascom prompted. "Quit pussyfootin' around. What'd she say?"

"There's a tough nut by the name of Rafe Dolan. Don't come here often, but when he does, everybody walks on eggshells. Musgrave and McCord won't even say his name out loud."

" 'Fraid he'll put a leak in their ticker, are they?"

Jordan nodded. "Hannah says he's mean as a snake. Way it sounds, he's got a bite to match."

"Lemme get this straight," Bascom said. "They're runnin' scared, so they dummy up where Dolan's concerned. What's that got to do with us?"

"Hannah told me they've been waiting for Dolan to show. When he does, they figured to make the introduction and see where it goes. They've got some idea he'd like our style."

"You mean, they think he'd take us on?"

"I suppose," Jordan said. "Leastways that's what the girl told me."

Bascom pondered a moment. "She say how big a gang he's got?"

"Just that he's the biggest in the Nations."

"She give you any details? Like where he operates mostly, or anything about his hideout?"

"Nope," Jordan admitted. "Fact is, she was half scared to death herself. Quick as she dropped his name, she took off like her skirt was on fire."

Bascom squinted, working his chaw. "Guess we'd never heard about him except she's sweet on you."

"What gave you that idea?"

"Hell, I ain't blind! Anytime you're around, she gets that mooncalf look on her face."

"That obvious, huh?"

"No more'n a sharp stick in the eye."

Jordan smiled. "Good thing one of us has a way with women. Otherwise we'd still be scratchin' for a lead."

"Better watch yourself," Bascom warned. "She'll likely try to get you in bed and ride your pony. Women always figure one favor deserves another."

"Why hell, Newt, if it comes to that, I'll sic her on you. What are friends for?"

Bascom grunted derisively. "Forget her and get back to business. How do we get a line on this Dolan?"

"Just for openers," Jordan tapped an ash off his cigarette, "I thought we'd try a little extortion."

"How's that again?"

"For all we know, hell could freeze over before Dolan puts in an appearance. By then, that Durham bull would be long gone."

"No argument there," Bascom said. "So what've you got in mind?"

Jordan turned to stare at the horses in the corral. He took a long drag, exhaling smoke. "Could be we're just grabbin' at straws. But something tells me Dolan's our man. We can't waste any more time. We've got to find him."

"So who we gonna extort? Somebody's gotta tell us where to look."

"Only one man fits the ticket—McCord."

Bascom liked it. "You're thinkin' we're all that stands between him and sudden death. Am I readin' you right?"

"On the money, pardner."

"When you figger to squeeze him?"

"No time like the present."

They walked back to the trading post. Inside, the dinner table was cleared and Musgrave was arranging goods on a shelf behind the counter. Through the rear doorway, they saw Hannah moving around in the kitchen. McCord was seated at the faro table, idly shuffling cards.

"Well, now," he said cordially. "You saved me from playing solitaire. Jolly old pharaoh awaits your pleasure."

Jordan and Bascom took their usual seats. McCord shuffled, allowed Bascom to cut, and placed the deck in the faro box. He paused, a cheroot wedged in the corner of his mouth, and waited for them to make their bets. Jordan tapped a marker on the layout, caught McCord's attention. He looked at them with a curious expression.

"What is it, Sam? Something wrong?"

"You might say that," Jordan observed. "Newt and me have been talkin' it over. We've come to the conclusion you're a goddamn tinhorn."

McCord's features betrayed nothing. "That's a serious allegation, Sam. Would you care to elaborate?"

"Spells out real simple. We're saying you're a card-sharp—a cheat."

There was a moment of leaden silence. McCord sat straighter in his chair, and his right hand shifted toward the edge of the table. They knew he carried a pistol in a shoulder holster and an over/under derringer secreted in his vest pocket. Jordan froze him with a look.

"Don't even think about it, Earl. I'm too fast for you."

McCord sat perfectly still. What he saw in Jordan's eyes was his own death warrant. At last, careful to make no sudden movements, he leaned forward on the table. His voice was controlled, oddly sardonic.

"Accusations are one thing, gentlemen. Proving it is another matter entirely."

"Like hell," Bascom said bluntly. "You deal seconds and you deal off the bottom. Caught on to it the first time we played."

McCord shrugged. "Your word against mine, Newt. That's hardly proof."

"The proof's right there in that faro box. You stripped the cards, most likely with a razor. Be real easy to show anybody how you done it."

"Indeed?" McCord's face was deadpan. "For a cattle rustler, you have an unusual knowledge of the gambler's art. Are you perhaps more than you pretend?"

"We're talkin' about you," Bascom informed him. "How you've hornswoggled all the boys hereabouts. You'd best think about your own skin."

"Are you threatening me with exposure?"

"Bet your lily-white ass we are! One peep from us and them dogs would be sicced on you *muy pronto*."

"They're rough customers," Jordan said quietly. "Even money whether they'd string you up or slice you into little pieces. Either way, you'd be worm-meat."

McCord's composure slipped. The thought of how his outlaw clientele would slowly and gleefully kill him was revolting. All the more so when he considered the loss of dignity he would suffer at their hands. His features blanched and he stared hollow-eyed across the table.

"What is it you want?"

Jordan glanced over his shoulder, ensuring that Musgrave was still absorbed with stocking the shelves. Then, hitching his chair forward, he lowered his voice. "We're interested in a rustler—Rafe Dolan."

McCord's eyes darted to the kitchen door. "Hannah told you," he said, more a statement than a question. "Until you arrived, she was my faithful bedmate. Apparently her allegiance depends on her carnal urges."

"Where we got the name doesn't matter. What we want from you is information on Dolan."

"You don't know what you're asking. Dolan would kill me in an instant if he knew I . . . talked."

Jordan wiggled his hand. "Dolan won't hear about it one way or another. So he's the least of your worries. Just keep thinkin' on what happens if we spread the word—about your fancy dealing."

"Christ," McCord sighed heavily. "Tell me something. Are you two lawmen?"

"No need for insults," Jordan said with mock indignation. "We've got our own reasons for asking about Dolan."

"Go ahead, then—ask."

"Where's his hideout?"

"I haven't the foggiest," McCord said wearily. "Dolan's quite secretive about that. His men never speak of it either."

Jordan stared at him hard. "Save yourself some grief, Earl. Don't lie to me."

"I honest to God have no idea. Somewhere north of here, because that's the direction they ride in from. Other than that, no one knows—including Will and Hannah."

"What do you think, Newt?" Jordan said.

Bascom pursed his mouth. "Way our luck's runnin', he's probably telling the truth. 'Course, if he's not, we can always feed him to the dogs."

"I swear to you," McCord assured them. "I just don't know. Dolan and his men keep their lips buttoned."

Jordan rubbed his jawbone. "How many men in Dolan's gang?"

"Offhand, I'd say seven or eight. They never come here in a group. Usually two or three, sometimes one by himself."

"Dolan ever show up by himself."

"No," McCord said with conviction. "Generally, two or three of his thugs are with him. He keeps his back covered."

"How often do they come here?"

"There's no set pattern. They come in for supplies, or to play cards and drink. From their conversation, I gather that Dolan lets them off the leash after they've pulled a job."

"When's the last time one of them was here?"

"As a matter of fact," McCord said thoughtfully, "the night before you arrived. Quite a coincidence, isn't it?"

"And before that?"

"A day or so, as I recall. Two of them came in."

"And Dolan—when was his last time?"

McCord reflected a moment. "Now that you mention it, almost a month. I'd say he's overdue."

Jordan saw no alternative. With Dolan's whereabouts unknown, they would have to wait until he rode into the trading post. And since the gangleader was overdue, that could be at any moment. His gaze fixed on McCord.

"Listen close," he said. "Any of the gang walks through the door—especially Dolan—you give us the high sign. Understood?"

"Yes, of course."

"One last thing," Jordan said tightly. "You tip our hand and I'll kill you on the spot. Take it as gospel."

"Likewise that," Bascom amended, "if you try cheatin' me at faro anymore."

Late that night, after the supper table was cleared, Hannah resumed her story of the Cherokee. McCord and Bascom kept themselves occupied at the faro layout. Jordan listened to her intently, a cigarette in his hand and one eye on the door. However compelling her story, his mind never strayed far from Rafe Dolan.

The Cherokee tribe, Hannah related, once occupied parts of Alabama, Georgia and Tennessee. In 1830, under pressure from white settlers, Congress passed the Indian Removal Bill. A legalized form of larceny, the legislation granted Western lands to the Five Civilized Tribes in exchange for their ancestral birthrights. Over the next several years, a total of 18,000 Cherokee were herded westward across what became known as the Trail of Tears. Of that number, more than 4,000 men, women and children perished before reaching Indian Territory. The Cherokee honored their memory by still referring to themselves as the *Tsalagi*.

When she finished, her father added a footnote. White men, Musgrave commented, were not allowed to own land in the Cherokee Nation, unless they married into the tribe.

He went on to say that men like Jordan and Bascom were welcome, because they, like the *Tsalagi*, refused to obey the white man's law. Jordan wondered whether it was merely a personal observation, or a sly proposal of marriage for Hannah. Either way, it had no bearing on the matter at hand. What he'd come to think of as The Case.

Of course, he told himself, The Case was going nowhere fast. Unless, or until, Rafe Dolan walked through the door. He smoked in silence, waiting for the door to open.

# FOURTEEN

The next morning everyone gathered around the table for breakfast. Hannah outdid herself with a spread of fried eggs, thick slices of ham, sourdough biscuits, and blackberry jam. She made a point of serving Jordan first, and kept casting fluttery glances his way during the meal. Will Musgrave pretended not to notice.

McCord was all too aware of the byplay. He sensed that something had changed overnight, particularly when Hannah studiously avoided looking at him. By her actions, there was no question in his mind that she and Jordan had somehow connected during the night. The loss of her affections was of no great consequence, though it ragged his pride. What grated most was that he'd lost not just his mistress, but his personal freedom as well, to the same man. Sam Jordan now held him hostage to events beyond his control.

The conversation around the table was curiously one-sided. Hannah gaily chirped on like a schoolgirl with her first party dress. She looked unusually radiant, and her eyes danced with unsuppressed merriment. Musgrave and Bascom concentrated on their food, and Jordan seemed uncomfortable with her constant chatter. McCord was more observer than participant, for none of the conversation was directed his way. He lit a cheroot as the meal ended, pouring himself another mug of coffee. When Jordan and Bascom headed toward the door, he toyed with the thought of killing them from behind. Yet he was no back-shooter, and the notion was quickly discarded.

Outside, Jordan paused to roll a cigarette. Bascom pulled out a plug of tobacco and bit off a chunk. He forked the fresh load into his cheek and began moistening it into a workable cud. Jordan started to return the muslin bag to his pocket, then stopped and stared at the Bull Durham label. He struck a match on his thumbnail, lighting his smoke.

"Funny thing," he said, holding the bag in the palm of his hand. "When we started out, I figured we'd find that bull in no time. You remember how they were trailing the critter at a walk?"

Bascom glanced at the Durham bull on the label. "Wish't I'd caught on to their tricks back there at Red Deer Creek. We would've saved ourselves a heap of time."

Their search had now consumed the better part of three weeks. What bothered them most was that the bull could have been trailed from Indian Territory to virtually any point on the compass. Even if Rafe Dolan was their man, there was no certainty that the bull was still being held in the Nations. For all they knew, Lord Ingram's Durham was long gone and far away.

"That's spilt milk now," Jordan said, exhaling a thin stream of smoke. "We've got to assume Dolan's our boy and hope he hasn't unloaded the bull."

"What if he has?" Bascom posed a disturbing question. "What then?"

"We find out who bought him and where to look next. Got no choice but to recover him, even if it takes till Christmas."

"Jesus Pesus Christ! Don't even talk like that. Come winter, we'd freeze our balls off dodgin' blue northers and blizzards. Makes my gonads shrivel up just thinkin' about it."

They walked down to the riverbank. The Verdigris swept past on its winding course southward. On the opposite shore, a hawk took wing off the branch of a tree and caught an updraft. Bascom watched silently as the hawk floated higher, silhouetted against the morning sun. Finally, his chaw thoroughly moistened, he spat a jet of tobacco juice.

"Let's just suppose," he speculated, "that Dolan shows up here. How you figger to play it?"

Jordan stared out across the river. "We let Musgrave perform the introductions. Hannah says he's primed to do it anyhow."

"What next?"

"Someway or another, we've got to get on the good side of Dolan. Set it up so he asks us to join his gang. He'd likely shy away if we did the asking."

Bascom nodded agreement. "So we euchre him into recruitin' us and we sign on. Then what?"

"Well, first off," Jordan noted, "we find out if he's got the bull. Until then, we really don't know what's what."

"And suppose Dolan don't show? Let's say it's only some of his boys—"

"There's no way to stop Musgrave from introducing us. But from what McCord says, none of Dolan's men will offer us a job. They just wouldn't risk it."

"Yeah, you're right," Bascom said. "Dolan would probably skin 'em alive. Leastways, that's how it sounds."

Jordan took a long pull on his cigarette. "McCord's got me curious," he said, watching the breeze take the smoke as he exhaled. "Wonder if Dolan's as tough as everybody makes him out. Lots of people get by on a reputation that's mostly hot air."

"You're like a gawddamn bulldog! Always wonderin' if you can cut the other feller down to size. Don't you tangle with Dolan till our job's done and over."

"Newt, we haven't even set eyes on the bastard yet. Why fret yourself when he might not even show?"

"Just suppose he don't," Bascom said. "Say it's one of the others instead. I take it you aim to follow him when he leaves?"

"Like a bloodhound," Jordan acknowledged. "Whatever and whichever, we can't afford to lose his trail. We've run out of time."

"And if we track him to Dolan's hideout?"

"We play it loose and fast. Do whatever needs doing."

"Howsoever, don't you go pickin' a fight with

Dolan. Don't make no nevermind whether he's hot air or Deadeye Dick. The job comes first."

"Newt, you worry too much. Startin' to sound like an old mother hen."

"Don't prod a hornet's nest, that's my motto."

The side door of the trading post opened. Hannah stepped out from the kitchen and tossed a pan of dirty dishwater into the yard. As she turned, she happened to glance down toward the river. She spotted Jordan and Bascom, who had looked around when the door opened. A girlish smile lighted her face and she waved happily to Jordan. Then she stepped back into the kitchen.

Bascom appeared troubled. "Guess you thought I didn't hear you sneak out of the room last night."

"You sleep too light for that. I figured you were awake."

"Hope to hell that gal don't cause us no problems. Way McCord talks, she's fickle as a firefly."

Jordan ditched his cigarette into the river. "She gave me an invite on the Q.T. just before we turned in. Under the circumstances, I couldn't hardly refuse."

"What d'you mean?"

"Wouldn't pay to get on her wrong side. She might try some damn fool nonsense when Dolan shows up. Not worth the risk."

"Ain't you the hero," Bascom said with a sly grin. "Sacrificed yourself just so's we wouldn't hit no snags. Remind me to give you a medal."

Jordan smiled. "All in the line of duty, Newt."

"Line of duty my dusty butt! Last time I heard, it was still called poontang."

"You always were a cynic."

"Well, Sam, I thank you for savin' the day. I shorely do."

"Anytime at all, Newt. No sacrifice too great."

Early that afternoon a lone man rode into the trading post. He was leading a packhorse, the canvas pack gear flat and empty. After dismounting, he left the horses ground-reined and went through the door. Will Musgrave greeted him with a broad grin.

"Clute! Long time no see. How you been?"

"Fair to middlin', I reckon. Yourself?"

"Never better, Clute. What can I do for you?"

"The boss sent me to fetch supplies. Here's the list."

Musgrave accepted the slip of paper. "Listen here, you've got time for a drink, don't you? Maybe a little cards?"

"That and whatever Hannah's fixin' for supper. I'm not expected back till mornin'."

"Good, good!"

Musgrave led him over to the faro table. The play was momentarily halted, with McCord seated across from Jordan and Bascom. McCord greeted the man by name, and Musgrave hastily performed introductions.

"Clute Johnson," he said, "this here's Sam Jordan and Newt Bascom. Texas boys, up this way for their health. You might say they're in your line of work."

Johnson evidenced no interest in pursuing the subject. He looked them over, then took a chair while Musgrave went for a fresh glass. He was whipcord-lean and wore a brace of pistols on crossed gun belts. Jordan noted that he seated himself where he could watch everyone at the table.

McCord removed the cards from the faro box. "Change of games," he said. "Clute doesn't care much for faro. Poker all right with you gentlemen?"

"Suits me," Jordan said, and Bascom readily agreed. As McCord began shuffling, he glanced across at Jordan with an almost imperceptible nod. He'd been asked for a high sign, and there was no question now that Clute Johnson was one of Dolan's men. He set the deck out for Johnson to cut.

"How's tricks, Clute?"

"No complaints."

"All the boys well, I trust?"

"Whyn't you forget the jabber? Just deal the cards."

"Five card stud," McCord said genially. "Three dollar limit, check and raise permitted. Everyone ante a dollar."

Johnson pulled a buckskin bag from his pocket and spilled gold coins onto the table. Jordan and Bascom, until now playing with markers, dug money from their pockets. McCord dealt, opening the game, one card in the hole and the other face up.

"Queen high," he said. "Your bet, Newt."

Johnson proved to be a wild bettor. As the game progressed, it became apparent that he unwisely chased busted straights and tried to better low pairs. Worse, he had no skill at reading the other players' cards and invariably attempted to bluff at the wrong times. He lost heavily, with a surly, begrudging manner.

Hardly an hour later, Johnson's pile of coins had dwindled to a single gold eagle. McCord was dealing straight cards, avoiding any sleight of hand. But luck fell to one side of the table, mainly to Bascom, and Johnson's attitude became increasingly sullen. When he lost another pot, he slammed his fist into the table.

"Goddammit, McCord!" he snarled. "You done set me up somehow. You're in cahoots with these jokers."

"Hold on, friend," Bascom said evenly. "Nobody rigged this game. Everything's on the up-and-up."

"I ain't your friend and I ain't no fool! I say you and McCord are workin' together."

"C'mon now, simmer down. Just because you had a run of bad luck—"

"You sorry sonovabitch. No luck to it! I been cheated."

"Anybody cheated you, it was yourself. You ain't much of a poker player."

Johnson's face mottled with rage. He kicked back his chair, clawing at the gun on his right hip. Bascom shaded him by a split second, pulling from the cross-draw holster while he was still seated. As Johnson cleared leather, Bascom fired from across the table. The slug struck Johnson beneath the breastbone and drove him into the wall. His eyes glazed and the cocked gun dropped from his hand. He slid down the wall, then toppled sideways to the floor.

Jordan rose and moved around the table. He knelt, checking the vein in Johnson's neck for a pulse. After a moment, he climbed to his feet, shook his head. "You put his lights out, Newt."

Bascom still sat with the pistol in his hand. "Jesus Christ," he said dumbly. "Why'd he pull an asinine stunt like that?"

"Guess we'll never know. He's through talkin'."

"I've done spoiled it, haven't I, Sam?"

"Wasn't your fault," Jordan said. "He made the fight."

"Yeah, maybe so," Bascom mumbled. "But what the hell we gonna do now? How're we gonna find Dolan?"

"Good question, Newt. Damn good question."

# FIFTEEN

**M**usgrave looked as though he'd been struck a hard blow. Hannah rushed from the kitchen and stood staring at the body with an expression of wild-eyed fright. After the gunshot, the silence in the room seemed almost deafening. The suddenness of death left them stunned, robbed of speech.

McCord was the only calm one in the room. He'd been surprised that Clute Johnson carried the argument to the extreme. No one had ever before pulled a gun during a card game at the trading post. Even more surprising was Bascom's quickness with a gun, his display of cool nerve. He had actually fired while still seated in his chair.

All in all, McCord told himself, the situation solved his most immediate problem. Rafe Dolan, if nothing else, was loyal to his men. Upon learning of Johnson's death, he would demand retribution, an eye for an eye. So Jordan and Bascom would be forced to hit the trail for parts unknown. Their departure would eliminate any possibility of McCord being exposed as a cheat. And Hannah, ever the opportunist, would gladly return to his bed. He thought the dead man had done him an enormous favor.

Musgrave at last recovered his wits. He crossed the room and stood staring down at the blood-splattered body. His expression, when he finally turned to Jordan and Bascom, was one of grave concern. "You've ripped it now," he said. "That was one of Rafe Dolan's men. Does the name mean anything to you?"

Jordan saw Hannah catch her breath. There was nothing to be gained by putting her at odds with her father. He decided to play dumb. "Who's Rafe Dolan?"

"The worst hard case in the Nations. He's a rustler and a killer and God knows what else. You have to get out of here right now."

"Hell with that," Jordan said. "Newt was just protectin' himself."

Bascom stood, holstering his pistol. "The sorry bastard pulled on me! What'd you expect me to do?"

"Doesn't matter," Musgrave said. "What counts is that you killed one of Dolan's boys. He'll come looking for you."

"Let him come!" Bascom said hotly, motioning to the body. "That scutter accused me of cheatin' and he done his damnedest to drill me. I was plumb within my rights."

Musgrave shook his head. "Dolan's not the sort who cares about right or wrong. He takes offense real easy—and this . . ."

The words trailed off as Musgrave cut his eyes to the dead man. There was a long moment of strained silence while they all stared at the body. At length, Hannah recovered her voice.

"Sam, listen to me," she said to Jordan. "I don't want you to leave, you know that. But I don't want to see you killed either. And if you stay, that's what will happen."

"Look here now," Jordan said stubbornly. "Newt and me have been in tight scrapes before. We generally manage to hold our own."

"Besides which," Bascom added, "why should we tuck tail and run? Wasn't our fault that peckerhead went loco."

Hannah's eyes went moist. "Why won't you listen? You haven't got a chance if you stay here!"

"She's right," Musgrave said. "You boys' pride will get you killed. We're just trying to help you."

Jordan glanced at McCord. "How about you, Earl? Think Dolan will take it all that personal?"

"No question of it," McCord said soberly. "And he won't come alone either. I'd say it's long odds, all in his favor."

"See what you mean," Jordan said. "Let Newt and me think about it. Meantime, we'll get the late Mr. Johnson planted. Don't suppose you've got a graveyard?"

"No need," Musgrave said hurriedly. "We'll take care of that."

"Nosirree," Bascom cut in. "We kill 'em, we bury 'em! Where's your shovel?"

Jordan took the legs and Bascom took the shoulders. While Musgrave held the door, they lugged the body outside. By the time they reached the woods behind the trading post, they were breathing heavily. After lowering the dead man to the ground, they took a moment to catch their breath.

"Helluva note," Bascom grouched. "All went wrong real sudden there. Didn't have no choice but to shoot him."

Jordan smiled. "Never saw you in better form, Newt. Johnson figured he had you cold."

"Goddamm dumb sonovabitch! You'd think he would've had more sense."

"Water under the bridge now. Dolan's the one we've got to worry about."

"Way they talk," Bascom commented, "we ain't got the chance of an icicle in hell. You think we ought to skedaddle?"

"That'd be the smart move," Jordan replied. "'Course, we've played into long odds before. Hate to come so far just to chuck the whole thing."

"Them's my sentiments exactly. Wouldn't want anybody back home to think we showed the white feather."

"Well, in a way, it speeds things along. We don't have to chase Dolan—he'll come to us."

Bascom spat, kicked up a puff of dust. "Way McCord talks, Dolan ain't likely to come alone. How d'you aim to handle it?"

"Guess it all depends," Jordan said. "We'll try to talk him around, and see how it goes. Maybe he's not the hothead everybody claims."

"And if he forces a fight?"

"I'll take him and you take whoever's closest."

Bascom studied on it. "Comes to a fight, I suspect

we can't trust Musgrave or McCord. You get the same feelin'?"

"Yeah, I do," Jordan said. "Whatever happens, don't let them get behind you. Odds are worse enough right now."

"You wouldn't mind a suggestion, would you?"

"What's that?"

"Hannah," Bascom said bluntly. "Think you oughta stay away from her tonight. We'd do well to take turns standin' watch."

Jordan looked at him. "You really think they'd try something stupid?"

"They're all scared outta their wits of Dolan. I can think of one surefire way they'd earn his good graces."

"Kill the gents that killed Clute Johnson, right?"

"Dolan would probably give 'em a real nice bounty."

"I dunno," Jordan said doubtfully. "They sounded pretty sincere, all that talk about us taking off."

"Mebbe so," Bascom allowed. "But we just decided we're stayin' put. That might change the way they look at things."

"Yeah, I suppose you're right. Wouldn't hurt to keep one eye open."

Musgrave walked toward them carrying a shovel. He stopped, handing the shovel to Bascom, and his gaze was drawn to the body. After a moment, he looked up at Jordan.

"Are you going to leave?"

"Way we see it, we've got no reason to run. We'll put it to Dolan so he understands."

"You're making a mistake we'll all regret."

Musgrave walked off, his head bowed. Jordan took out the makings, sprinkled tobacco into a paper. He thought one eye open would be wise all around.

Bascom began digging a hole.

By noontime the next day, a shroud of tension hung over the trading post. Hannah rattled dishes when she served the midday meal. Musgrave and McCord were reduced to an edgy, tight-lipped silence. There was no longer any conversation with their unwanted guests.

Jordan and Bascom took chairs facing the door. They were uncomfortably aware of the hard feelings, and the palpable sense of fear around the table. Since yesterday, they had made it a point not to turn their backs on anyone, including Hannah. Their distrust was not lost on the others.

Everyone waited with growing unease. They recalled Clute Johnson's casual remark from yesterday. Sent to fetch supplies, he'd been expected back sometime this morning. When he failed to return, there was no question that a search party would be sent to inquire at the trading post. Whether or not Rafe Dolan would lead the search party was open to speculation. Musgrave, along with McCord and Hannah, clearly feared the worst.

Jordan was under no illusions about their attitude. When push came to shove, they wouldn't hesitate to denounce the two Texans. He understood their fear, and anticipated their rush to distance themselves from Johnson's death. Unlike them, his greater fear was that Dolan would simply dispatch some gang members to check on the missing man. Last night, in the privacy of their sleeping quarters, he and Bascom had discussed the point at length. Their concern was that Dolan wouldn't bother himself with joining the search party.

Dealing with Dolan was one thing. Dealing with other gang members posed a whole new set of problems. Even if they captured the search party, it was questionable that any of them would betray Dolan, which would aggravate the situation without providing a solution. What they needed was the location of the gang's hideout.

Their concern proved to be ungrounded. Shortly after noon, three men walked through the door. The one in the lead was of medium height, with a muscular build and sharp gray eyes. Though in his early thirties, he was a man of commanding presence, someone accustomed to being obeyed. The reaction of Musgrave and the others, all of them suddenly quite still, left no doubt as to his identity. Rafe Dolan had arrived.

Jordan was standing at the end of the counter, opposite Musgrave. He finished rolling a cigarette, and lit it as the three men crossed the room. Over the flare of the match, he nodded to Bascom, who was seated at the faro table with McCord. Hannah stood in the kitchen doorway, arms folded over her breasts, hugging herself. Dolan halted before the

counter, flanked by his men. His eyes swept over
Jordan and Bascom, assessing them at a glance. He
nodded to Musgrave.

"You seen Johnson?" he asked in a curt voice. "I
sent him down here yesterday to get supplies."

"Rafe—" Musgrave faltered, beads of sweat on
his forehead.

"Got some bad news," Jordan interjected quietly.
"We buried your boy out back late yesterday. Even
said some words over him."

Dolan turned from the counter. "Who are you?"

"Jordan. Sam Jordan."

"How'd Johnson come to get buried?"

"Lead poisoning," Jordan said. "He pulled a gun
over a little dispute about cards. Everybody here
will vouch for it—he started the fight."

"And you killed—"

Dolan began his draw in midsentence. His men,
moving in unison, were only a beat behind. But as
their hands touched the gun-grips, a metallic whirr
sounded throughout the room. At the faro table,
Bascom leveled a cocked pistol, the sights centered
on Dolan. There was an instant of tomblike silence
as the three outlaws stood with their guns half
drawn.

"That's my partner," Jordan told them. "Like you
to meet Newt Bascom."

"You're real cute," Dolan said, releasing his gun-
butt. "Had us boxed the minute we walked in here,
didn't you?"

"Figured you might take the news the wrong way.

Thought it'd plumb be a waste, anybody else got killed."

"So we got ourselves a standoff. What happens now?"

"Well, you lost a man," Jordan said, "and Newt and me are pretty fair hands with a long rope. We're lookin' for work."

"You're joking!" Dolan said, astounded. "You're asking me for a job?"

"Know it sounds a little outlandish. 'Specially since we put your boy under. But, what the hell, you're short of help and we need the work."

"You got brass, I'll give you that." Dolan fixed Musgrave with a penetrating look. "What about it, Will? Are they tellin' the truth?"

Musgrave bobbed his head. "Saw it with my own eyes, Rafe. Johnson forced the fight and got himself killed. Wasn't no rhyme or reason to it."

Dolan's gaze swung around. "Jordan, I like your style. 'Course, if it turns out you and your partner aren't on the owlhoot—you're dead men."

"Told you the straight goods. There's wanted dodgers on us down in Texas."

"Then tell your buddy to lower the hammer. He's making me nervous."

"Does that mean we're hired on?"

"Just told you so, didn't I?"

Jordan stuck out his hand, grinning broadly, and pumped Dolan's arm. Bascom earred the hammer down and holstered his gun. He rose from the faro table, aware that relief had spread across the room.

As he approached the counter, Dolan gave him a critical once-over. The gangleader wagged his head.

"You boys killed a good man. Clute Johnson could steal anything that wasn't nailed down."

Bascom laughed. "You got yourself a fair swap, Mr. Dolan. We've stole some things that *was* nailed down!"

# SIXTEEN

**R**afe Dolan proved to be an engaging rogue. He bought three rounds of drinks in the time it took to fill his supply order. Hannah tended the bar while her father stored goods in the canvas packs. No one mentioned that the order had gone unfilled due to the untimely demise of Clute Johnson. The conversation was instead rather genial.

The men with Dolan were introduced as Buster Fenton and Arnie Grove. For the most part, they sipped whiskey and allowed their boss to do the talking. McCord was invited to join the group for drinks, and he, too, kept his lip buttoned. Jordan and Bascom were made the center of attention, with Dolan drawing them out in casual conversation. His manner was one of idle curiosity.

Jordan and Bascom were aware that they were being subjected to subtle interrogation. Dolan's questions were roundabout, never openly probing or suspicious. Yet he kept the focus on Texas, and his questions, skillfully couched, were directed to their activities as rustlers. What he asked, particularly about cattle brands, indicated that he was familiar with ranching outfits throughout the Lone Star State. He grilled them in a crafty, understated tone.

However artfully done, Jordan was by no means fooled. The conversation was meant to determine whether they were, in fact, on the run from Texas lawmen. A minor lapse, or anything that sounded out of order, and they would have failed the test. He had no doubt that the penalty for failure would be swift and permanent. Dolan was engaging in the way a grifter cons a mark, always looking for weakness. A wrong answer would have gotten them killed.

An hour or so later, Musgrave returned from loading the packhorse. Buster Fenton and Arnie Grove were clearly disappointed that their stay was being cut short. A night at the trading post, drinking and trying their luck at McCord's faro game, was their obvious preference. The fact that they made no protest spoke further as to the true character of their boss. Dolan commanded simply by stating what he intended, or what he wanted done. Everyone else fell into line with no thought of questioning his orders. He operated on the principle that when he said "frog," other people jumped.

Outside, Jordan and Bascom found that Musgrave had already saddled their horses. Hannah came to the door and watched with a wistful look as Jordan mounted. He nodded to her, aware that the exchange was not lost on Dolan. Then the gangleader reined his horse out of the yard and turned upriver. Fenton and Grove brought up the rear, with Grove leading the packhorse. Though no order had been passed, it was clear that an unspoken message had gone out from Dolan. The new men were to ride in the middle, under constant observation.

A short distance upstream Dolan turned in his saddle. He grinned at Jordan, nodding back at the trading post. "Appears you caught Hannah's eye."

Jordan gave him a tomcat smile. "Women are my mortal weakness. Never could resist 'em."

"Often been tempted by Hannah myself. She's got that look about her."

"Known lots of women, but none like her. She's wilder than a bucket of red ants."

Dolan cocked one eye. "McCord's always had dibs on Hannah up till now. Seems like he'd figure you jumped his claim."

"Yeah, maybe so," Jordan said. "'Course, there wasn't much he could've done about it. She made her choice."

"Wonder he didn't call you out. McCord's a pretty fair hand with a gun."

"Guess he knew better."

Dolan laughed. "Think you could take him, huh?"

"I'd be obliged to try."

"Dropped the hammer on somebody before, have you?"

"Well—" Jordan motioned with his off hand. "Let's just say, nobody I'd admit to."

"I like a man with a tight lip. You ought to fit in real good with our bunch."

Dolan swiveled around in his saddle. Watching him from the rear, Jordan was impressed by the gang-leader. So far he'd seen two sides of Rafe Dolan. One was the hard case who ruled with an iron fist and commanded respect, not to mention outright fear, from those who knew him. The other was an amiable, soft-spoken man who could lull people into thinking he was friendly and easygoing. Jordan told himself that the former seemed closer to the truth than the latter. Yet he wondered if there weren't other sides still to be revealed.

Rafe Dolan appeared to be a man of many parts.

Shortly after sundown they rounded a dogleg bend in the river. Ahead was a crude log structure, with a ramshackle look of impermanence. Off to one side was a large holding pen, constructed of stout timbers, quartered by cross-timbers into four sections. By the time they rode into the clearing, nightfall had settled over the land.

Jordan placed the hideout some ten miles upstream from the trading post. The door opened and a man stood framed in a shaft of lamplight. As they dismounted, Jordan and Bascom sensed animals milling about in the holding pen. But in the darkness they were unable to make out distinct shapes, though they heard the low, snuffling sound of horses. The question in both their minds was whether or not a Durham bull occupied one of the holding pens. The answer would have to await daylight.

Dolan ordered Fenton and Grove to unsaddle the horses. He then led Jordan and Bascom toward the cabin, into the spill of light. The man standing in the doorway was tall and sledge-shouldered, with the lean flanks of a horseman. His features were hard, all rough planes set off by a splayed nose and high cheekbones. His skin was a shade lighter than saddle-leather, and there seemed little doubt that he was a half-breed of some variety. He stepped aside as Dolan moved through the door.

The cabin smelled like a wolf den. On the left, just inside the door, was a washstand with a faded mirror. Strewn on the floor was a jumble of war bags, filthy clothes, and weathered saddle gear. A set of double bunks stood end to end along opposite walls, and a rough-hewn table, flanked by a potbelly stove, occupied the central living area. Beyond the table, at the far end of the room, was a wood cook-stove and shelves packed with canned goods. There were two men seated at the table and another bent over the cookstove.

"Boys," Dolan said, motioning over his shoulder. "I want you to meet Sam Jordan and Newt Bascom." He indicated the men at the table. "These two no-accounts are Ed Urschel and Jack Langham. And that's Jake Irvin back at the stove. Better known as Doc."

The half-breed closed the door and crossed the room. Dolan nodded to him with a faint smile. "This here's my right arm and the best horse-stealer in the Injun Nations. Meet Luther Hall."

Never taking his eyes off them, Hall spoke to Dolan. "Where's Johnson?"

"Dead," Dolan said bluntly. "I'll tell you about it over supper. C'mon, Doc, what's with the grub?"

"Just about ready," Irvin called from the stove. "Grab yourselves a seat."

Fenton and Grove trooped in as a black iron kettle was placed in the middle of the table. The men slopped a greasy stew from the kettle onto tin plates while Irvin pulled a large pan of corn bread from the oven. They ate like a ravenous pack, grunting and belching as though gorging themselves on a fresh kill. Yet their eyes were on Dolan, who sat at the head of the table, sopping corn bread in stew gravy. At the other end, Hall ate with unhurried deliberation, watching Jordan and Bascom. His expression was wooden.

"What happened," Dolan said around a mouthful of cornbread, "Johnson got himself drilled in an argument over cards." He waved a spoon at Bascom. "Newt here done the dirty deed."

Hall stared down the table. "What kind of argument?"

"No offense intended," Bascom said, "but Johnson was a sore loser. Damn fool went for his gun."

"And you shot him?"

"Wasn't a helluva lot of choice. Way it worked out, it was him or me."

Hall's gaze shifted to Dolan. "Something don't sit right here. Why'd you hire 'em—after they killed Clute?"

"Well, Luther," Dolan said in a mocking tone, "Sam convinced me it was a smart move. We were short a man and these boys were handy. So they tell me, they've got some experience in our line of business."

Jordan suddenly saw where the conversation was headed. Luther Hall was Dolan's lieutenant and chief enforcer. His job was to keep the crew in line and perform any dirty work required. The way Jordan read it, he and Bascom were to be subjected to one last test. A glimmer of an idea popped into his head, and he saw that it had possibilities. Hall's voice intruded on the thought and he looked up to find himself riveted by a churlish scowl.

"Where're you from?"

"West of Fort Worth," Jordan said. "Worked mainly along the Brazos."

"What outfits are out that way?"

"Lazy S and the Rocking K are the biggest. Whole slew of small outfits."

Hall glared at him. "And you claim you rustled their stock?"

"Bet your ass," Jordan said. "Took off before they could put a rope around our necks. Those folks are plumb serious when it comes to cows."

"You got any proof of that?"

"Don't need proof, friend. You just heard me say it."

Hall's eyes went steely. "What if I said your word's not good enough?"

"Then I'd tell you to saddle up and ride on down there. First tree you come to, look for a wanted dodger. You'll find Newt and me nailed to the bark."

Dolan laughed. "Told you he was a talker, didn't I?" He shoved his plate away, motioning to Bascom. "Newt, you probably noticed we've got only eight bunks. Since you drilled Johnson, then by rights, his bunk goes to you. Sam will have to make do with the floor."

"Anything you say," Bascom agreed. "I ain't particular."

"What d'you think?" Dolan said to Hall. "Sounds fair, doesn't it? Spoils of war makes it Newt's bunk."

Jordan sensed that the remark was meant to goad Hall. The half-breed pushed back from the table and kicked his chair aside. As he started around Bascom's side of the table, Jordan rose and stepped clear of his chair. He regarded Hall with great calmness.

"What's your problem, friend?"

"You," Hall said in a raspy voice. "Time you got your wagon fixed."

"You're welcome to try."

They met in the open space between the table and the bunks. Hall uncorked a haymaker, and Jordan ducked under the blow. Before he could recover a left hook sent him reeling backward. The brassy taste of blood filled his mouth, and he was momentarily amazed by the half-breed's speed. He feinted with his shoulder, halting Hall's advance, and circled toward the table. Then he bobbed and weaved, purposely lowering his guard.

The tactic suckered Hall into a sweeping roundhouse. Jordan slipped inside and struck two splintering punches. Hall staggered, shook his head like a man who had walked into cobwebs, and Jordan landed a hard, clubbing right squarely between the eyes. The impact buckled Hall and he slammed upright into one of the bunks. He wavered a moment, then his eyes glazed, and he slid to the floor. A streamer of blood seeped from his nose down over his mouth. He was out cold.

Jordan turned back to the table. His eyes swept the men seated there. "Anybody else care to try his luck?"

No one took the offer. The gang seemed stunned by the swiftness with which he'd whipped Hall. Even Dolan took a moment to regain himself, staring in disbelief at his fallen lieutenant. Jordan pulled out the makings and rolled a smoke. He struck a match, lit the cigarette, and resumed his seat at the table. Dolan looked at him with new respect.

"You're pretty handy with your fists."

Bascom snorted. "He ain't bad with a gun neither."

"All that," Dolan said lightly, "and a ladies' man too. You're a regular jack-of-all-trades."

Jordan grinned. "You got a job needs doing, Newt and me are your boys."

Luther Hall groaned and rolled over on his side. Dolan studied him a moment with an odd, somewhat detached expression. Then he smiled at his two most recent recruits.

"I think you gents have found yourselves a home."

# SEVENTEEN

The next morning Doc Irvin slapped together breakfast. He kept one skillet sizzling with rough-cut slabs of beefsteak. At the same time, he worked another skillet with doughy flapjacks. A galvanized coffee pot bubbled with what was commonly tagged as "six-shooter" coffee. When it was thick enough to float a six-shooter, it was fit to drink.

Along with the other men, Jordan and Bascom took turns in the one-hole privy out behind the cabin. Since the privy was in the opposite direction, there was no excuse for them to inspect the stock pens. They returned to the cabin as Irvin began loading plates with food. The steaks were tough, the flapjacks went soggy with molasses syrup, and the coffee was strong enough to peel paint. The gang went at it like dogs jumping a gut-wagon.

Bascom chewed on a hunk of beefsteak until it was reduced to pulp. He washed it down with coffee, smacking his lips in a grimace, and looked at Irvin. "Doc, was you ever a chuck-wagon cook?"

Irvin turned from the stove. "Never had the honor. What makes you ask?"

"You got the knack, that's all. Takes talent to do a job like that on beef."

Irvin was short and stumpy, with salt-and-pepper hair. He cocked one eye in a baleful glare. "You complaining about my cookin'?"

"Not sayin' it's tough," Bascom remarked, poking the steak with his fork. "Just hope I don't break a molar."

Some of the men burst out laughing. Buster Fenton paused, his mouth stuffed with flapjacks, and ruefully shook his head. "Newt, what you just broke was Doc's rule."

"What rule's that?"

"Anybody gripes about the vittles has to wash dishes for a whole day."

"Ain't fair!" Bascom protested. "I only signed on yesterday."

"Don't matter," Irvin cackled. "Rules is rules."

Jordan watched the byplay with an amused smile. In cowcamps across the West, one of the chief forms of entertainment was in ragging the cook. On occasion, when the insults became too burdensome, cooks had been known to lace the food with castor oil. A case of the trots generally taught a crew of cowhands to mind their manners. For Jordan, there was yet another point of interest about the byplay this morning. He idly wondered why the gang's cook was called Doc.

After breakfast, the men trooped outside. Jordan noted that Hall was unusually quiet, and kept his distance. Since the fight last night, the half-breed even treated the other men with a certain gruff tolerance. Yet Jordan wasn't fooled. A bully never forgot or forgave, and one whipping rarely got the job done. He sensed that Hall's hostility simmered just beneath the surface. All it would take was an opportune moment, particularly from the rear, to trigger some form of retaliation. He reminded himself to watch his back.

Dolan's attitude merely aggravated the situation. He personally led Jordan and Bascom on a tour of the stock pens. A vain man, he took inordinate pride in his operation. On one side of the pens, two quarter-sections were devoted to horses. On the other side, each quarter-section housed a blooded bull. In the nearest pen was a Hereford, commonly called whiteface because of the wine-red coat and distinctive white from forehead to nose. The pen on the farthest side housed a powerfully built Durham.

Jordan paused to build a smoke. While Bascom engaged Dolan in conversation, he took his time rolling the cigarette. Holding the muslin bag, he compared the Bull Durham label to the bull in the enclosure. The markings and conformation of the bull on the label were an exact match for the bull that stood watching them with a wary eye. On closer inspection, he saw that the bull's left horn was curved in the same shape as the bull in Lord Ingram's painting. The clincher was the steel ring threaded through the bull's nose. There was no doubt whatever about the identity of the bull. He was looking at Homer.

The bull turned away as he popped a match and lit his cigarette. Over the flame he saw something that at once baffled and intrigued him. All stock on the Circle I spread, Lord Ingram's ranch, bore the ⟨ I ⟩ brand. But the bull in the enclosure was now branded with ⟨ III ⟩ Instead of Circle I, the brand would be read by any cattleman as Circle Three. Jordan snuffed his match, trying to get a closer look at the brand. Then the bull ambled to the far side of the enclosure, and the distance was too great. Still, whatever the brand, he was nonetheless certain that he'd found Homer. No two bulls could have a curved horn that was an exact look-alike.

Dolan led them to one of the horse pens. He stopped, motioning to the milling animals. "What d'you think of that?"

Jordan and Bascom peered through the railings. The horses were clearly blooded stock, a Morgan and several thoroughbreds among them. The brands were a mixed lot, none from any of the cattle outfits in western Texas. Bascom examined the stock with a critical eye.

"Not bad," he said, shifting his chaw. "Fact is, them are mighty fine ponies."

"Prime horseflesh," Dolan said proudly. "I don't deal in nothin' else. Prime horseflesh and imported bulls."

Bascom looked dubious. "You sayin' that's all you go after—the good stuff?"

"Tell you my motto," Dolan said. "If you're gonna steal, then steal only the best. You get hung as quick for rustlin' a scrub cow as you do a prize bull."

"So you're a sorta specialist, is that it?"

"Not to sound highfalutin, but I'm what you might call a discriminating thief. Cream of the crop and nothin' less."

"Don't that beat all," Bascom said, wagging his head in wonder. "But lemme ask you something. Ain't it hard to unload all this prize stock? Seems like people would ask lots of questions."

Dolan laughed. "I'm fixin' to show you boys a miracle. Hall and his crew brought these horses in just yesterday. Stole the whole bunch off of outfits down in eastern Texas."

"What's that got to do with a miracle?"

"Just hide and watch. You're not gonna believe your eyes."

While they were talking, the other men had gone about what appeared to be a routine drill. A branding fire was kindled and thick stakes were driven into the ground several feet apart. A wooden bucket, with a rag dauber fastened to a stick, was positioned away from the heat of the fire. Doc Irvin emerged from the cabin carrying lengths of heavy-gage wire and a lip twist. He nodded to the men.

Buster Fenton roped a blooded stallion and choused him from the pen. As Urschel swung the gate closed, Grove snaked a lariat around the stallion's rear hooves and Langham roped the front hooves. The horse was thrown to the ground and the men swarmed over him. Within seconds, his legs, front and rear, were lashed to the stakes. Hall held his head eared down, while Fenton and Langham kept his hindquarters from thrashing. The stallion was securely anchored.

Grove stepped in with the twist. He attached the rope loop to the horse's lower lip, then began turning the wooden handle like a tourniquet. The pain, intensifying with every turn, quickly distracted the stallion from all else. He stopped thrashing with a final turn of the twist, effectively immobilized on the ground.

Doc Irvin pulled a length of wire, now cherry-red, out of the fire. He moved forward and stood for a moment studying the LX on the stallion's flank. Then, with the utmost care, he positioned the wire and laid it over the brand. The smell of burnt hair and scorched flesh filled the air, and an instant later he moved back, inspecting his handiwork. The hot wire, as if by magic, had transformed LX into ⊠⊠.

After tossing the wire aside, Irvin collected the bucket. He stirred the contents, which appeared thick as axle grease and had the strong odor of liniment. With a quick stroke of the dauber, he spread a dark, pasty layer across the new brand. Finished, he nodded to himself and turned away. Led by Hall, the men unstrapped the stallion and herded him back into the pen. The entire operation had taken less than five minutes.

Jordan and Bascom had watched quietly. There was no second chance when altering a brand, and they were visibly impressed by Irvin's deft touch. Even more impressive was the hot wire, a technique far more effective than the running iron used by most rustlers. The original LX on the stallion had been converted into Box Double X, and altered so

cleverly that no one would give it a second glance.
They had to admire Irvin's crafty eye for detail.

Dolan nudged Bascom in the ribs. "What'd I tell
you? Don't that qualify as a miracle?"

"You bet'cha," Bascom said slowly. "Gawd-
damnedest thing I ever seen."

"You see now why we call him Doc. Not a saw-
bones between here and St. Louie who could perform that operation."

"That's a new one on me, his trick with the wire.
Only way I ever knowed was with a runnin' iron."

Dolan nodded. "Never once had anybody question his work. Horse or cow, it works like a charm."

Jordan began rolling a fresh smoke. "What's that
dope he uses, the stuff in the bucket?"

"Doc's secret recipe. He won't tell nobody the
mix. Cures the brand clean as a baby's butt in a couple of weeks."

"You sayin' it'll fool brand inspectors?"

"Christ himself couldn't tell it'd been touched!"

"Damn slick," Jordan said with admiration.
"Guess that makes it a sight easier to move the
stock. Sell 'em off in Dodge or somewheres, and
nobody the wiser."

The remark was designed to work on Dolan's
peacock pride. His chest expanded under the praise,
and he took their arms, walking them off to one
side. He waited until another horse had been
choused from the pen and the crew was occupied altering a brand. Then he lowered his voice.

"You boys got style," he said. "I like the way you

stood up to me when you killed Clute Johnson. And whippin' Hall's ass was a nifty piece of work. We're gonna get along just fine."

"Tell you the truth," Jordan said, playing the part. "We're happy as a couple of pigs in mud. You've got the smoothest operation we ever run across."

"Hell, you haven't seen the half of it. No way on God's green earth we're ever gonna get caught. I put together this operation like clockwork."

Dolan proudly elaborated on the details. Some four years past, in 1872, the Missouri, Kansas & Texas Railroad had laid track through the Nations. The railway extended from the Kansas border on a due south line through Indian Territory, and crossed the Red River into Texas. The railroad's cumbersome name had been shortened to "Katy" and the line now provided shipping access north and south. The railhead in the Cherokee Nation was located in Vinita, a whistle-stop settlement some thirty miles northeast of the gang's hideout. After the altered brands were cured, the rustled stock was trailed to Vinita.

The altered brands, Dolan went on, were all fake. Doc Irvin was careful to create nothing that could be found in registered brand books. For every animal, a bogus bill of sale was drafted, based on the new brand and a totally fictitious owner. The livestock was then shipped by railroad to a network of crooked dealers, in south Texas. The altered brands, coupled with the great distances involved, effectively erased any clue as to the livestock's original ownership. The stolen animals appeared legitimate and were easily sold to unsuspecting ranchers. The operation was foolproof.

"Don't like to brag," Dolan concluded, "but we get top dollar for blooded stock. That's why I'm choosy about what we steal."

Jordan and Bascom had to admire the man's cunning. Dolan had organized a masterful operation, with a logistical maze that made the stolen livestock virtually untraceable. There was a touch of genius to the whole scheme.

"Holy smokes," Bascom said with genuine awe. "That's plumb foxy. No other word for it."

"Damned if it's not," Jordan readily agreed. "These livestock dealers down in south Texas—how many you got?"

"Just four," Dolan said. "Handpicked 'em myself. Never a worry there, either. They know I'd kill 'em if they peep a word."

"When's your next shipment?"

"Day after tomorrow." Dolan motioned at the stock pens. "Doc figures that Durham's brand ought to be cured by then. Guaranteed to fetch big money."

Jordan forced a smile. But he dared not look at Bascom. They were both thinking the same thought. What amounted to a deadline. Day after tomorrow.

# EIGHTEEN

**B**y late morning the work was completed. The newly stolen horses had been doctored with fresh brands and returned to the stock pen. The gang loafed around awaiting the noonday meal.

Dolan, despite an occasional effort at modesty, welcomed the opportunity to brag. He made no pretense about his two new recruits. They were the kind of men he liked, tough and resourceful, willing to accommodate anyone who crossed them. And they were eager listeners, openly impressed by all he'd achieved. He went on like a professor lecturing to wide-eyed students.

"Take Doc, there," he said at one point. "Put his brains in a jaybird and the bastard would fly backwards. But he's a pure marvel with that hot wire."

Jordan and Bascom watched as Irvin walked toward the cabin. After a moment, Bascom spat a streak of tobacco juice. "Where'd you find him?"

"Funny thing about Doc. He was stealin' cows all by his lonesome. A couple here and a couple there. Just enough to keep him in grub and whiskey."

"Wasn't interested in the money?"

"Not all that much. He figured rustlin' was easier than steady work."

Bascom grunted. "Beats the hell outta thirty a month and found."

"My sentiments exactly," Dolan said. "Live high off the hog and let the other fellow pay the freight."

"Not being nosy," Jordan asked, "but how long you been in the business?"

"Close to three years. 'Course, most of that time I was just a common cow thief. Went big time when I stumbled across Doc."

"You talkin' about his trick with the wire?"

"Nothin' less." Dolan chuckled, shook his head. "Him and his wire take all the risk out of it. Never had anybody question his work. Stock inspectors, lawdogs, you name it!"

Jordan rolled a cigarette. "How'd he come up with the idea—hot wire?"

"Says a Mexican bandito showed him the trick. I halfway suspect that's pure hogwash. He don't speak a word of Mex."

"Even if he don't," Bascom said, "he's a purdee artist. Why'd his wire convince you to go big time?"

"Hell, it's foolproof," Dolan told him. "Why steal ordinary cows when it's just as easy to steal prime stuff? Lots less work and a helluva lot more money."

"Why do you say it's easier? Seems like it'd be riskier stealin' blooded stock. Folks tend to keep a closer watch on their prize stuff."

Dolan nodded across the clearing. Luther Hall and the other men were seated outside the cabin. "I come across Hall not long after I met Doc. You might say he's an artist in his own right. Never saw a man his equal with stock."

"How so?"

"Guess it's the Injun in him. He whispers real quiet, and gets them gentled down, and they'll follow him anywhere. He's like a ghost, the way he works. In and out, and nobody the wiser."

Jordan saw it now. The puzzle was comprised of four pieces. Doc Irvin and his hot wire. Luther Hall, who could spellbind animals. The Nations, where an outlaw found absolute sanctuary. And the fourth piece was the organizational genius of Rafe Dolan. He'd put it all together and added a new wrinkle to rustling. They stole only purebred stock.

"Only one trouble," Dolan mused aloud. "Hall's got a mighty high opinion of himself. Sometimes he forgets who runs this outfit."

Jordan took a drag, exhaled smoke. "Then you weren't put out when I boxed his ears?"

"Christ, no," Dolan said quickly. "I've had to take him down a peg or two myself every so often. Some people just have to be reminded of their place."

The comment was revealing. Jordan sensed that he and Bascom were a welcome addition to the gang. Dolan planned to use them as a buffer against Hall. In effect, a new means had been found to keep the half-breed in his place. Dolan would no longer have to dirty his own hands. Which explained why he'd spent the morning with them, taken them into his confidence. He wanted a check and balance against his upstart lieutenant, Luther Hall.

"I gotta take a leak," Dolan said. "See you boys when Doc has dinner fixed."

Jordan and Bascom watched as he headed toward the outhouse. When he was out of earshot, Bascom let out a muffled snort. "There goes one tricky sonovabitch."

"No two ways about it," Jordan agreed. "He plays all the angles, all the time. His mind never stops clickin'."

"What was he aimin' at with that last go-round? The part about Hall?"

"I've got a hunch Hall's been getting too big for his britches. Dolan don't want to kill him because he's a wizard with rustled stock. But we show up, and he sees an easy way out. He'll use us to whittle Hall down a notch or two."

Bascom spat, raising a puff of dust on the ground. "Bastard plays a sharp game, don't he?"

"Sharp and shrewd," Jordan said. "Takes real savvy to organize the operation he's got here. Closest thing I've ever seen to a lead-pipe cinch."

"Way it appears, he only rustles stock from the Panhandle and the north part of Texas. That gives him a straight run back into Indian Territory. Shore reduces the chances of gettin' caught."

"Not to mention nobody would be fool enough to track him into the Nations—except us."

Bascom jerked his chin around the clearing. "Bet the U.S. Marshals ain't got no inkling about this place. Like as not, they never heard of Dolan."

"Stands to reason," Jordan said. "Dolan lays low and never puts himself in the limelight. Wouldn't doubt he intends to retire a rich man in a couple of years."

"How much you think he gets for rustled stock?"

"Well, first off, he doesn't have to unload it at bargain rates. Once Doc does his miracle with the wire, it's all honest goods. So it's like he said— nothing but top dollar."

Bascom gummed his chaw. "And we know that Durham will fetch five thousand on the open market."

"Horses go for less," Jordan noted. "But that bunch in the pens will likely bring five thousand or more. Adds up real quick."

"Dolan uses his noodle, that's for sure. Think what the tally would be if he ships this many head every month."

They stared at each other a moment. Jordan rolled his eyes. "Christ, that's close to two hundred thousand a year."

"And we're pullin' down a hundred a month to get shot at!"

"What'd you think, he whacks off half for the gang and his dealers down in Texas? That still leaves him pretty near a hundred thousand."

"Way he lives," Bascom observed, "it shore don't show. Wonder where he's got it squirreled away."

"Short ride to Kansas," Jordan said. "Or Arkansas, for that matter. Banks don't ask how you come by cash money."

"Who you reckon collects from them livestock dealers?"

"I just suspect it's Dolan himself. Once a month

down and back on the train. Probably collects for last month when he delivers a new batch of stock."

"Yeah, probably," Bascom acknowledged. "And like he said, them dealers ain't about to welsh on the money. They know he'd put their lights out."

"Why welsh?" Jordan remarked. "They're unloading stock with papers and brands that nobody questions. Too good a deal to play loose with Dolan."

"Sweet, all right. Sweet as sugar."

Jordan rolled a fresh cigarette. He lit up and they casually strolled around the stock pens. On the far side their pace slowed as they passed the Durham bull. Bascom wrinkled his brow in a question.

"You figure Hall's the one that stole our bull?"

"Wouldn't be surprised, him being a half-breed. Way we got thrown off at Red Deer Creek would've done any Indian proud."

"Homer," Bascom grunted, casting a glance at the bull. "Helluva name for a critter that big."

"All the same, he's our bull. Hall probably took hold of that nose ring and waltzed him right out of the stall."

"Speakin' of Hall," Bascom said thoughtfully. "You'd better watch yourself real close. He might be fixin' to get back at you for the licking he took."

"We won't be around long enough to find out."

"Why not?"

"You heard Dolan. They're trailin' Homer over to railhead day after tomorrow."

"How d'you aim to stop 'em?"

"We're gonna steal him back."

"We are?" Bascom blinked owlishly. "When, just exactly?"

Jordan smiled. "Tonight."

Bascom's mouth popped open. Before he could frame a reply, Doc Irvin called the men to dinner. The noon meal was sparse and hasty, with warmed-over corn bread, a pot of beans laced with cayenne pepper, and another brew of six-shooter coffee. None of the men offered comment, for they remembered that Doc's rule had been imposed only that morning. Bascom got the honor of scrubbing pots and washing dishes when they were through.

Once the table was cleared, the poker game started. A ritual of sorts, the afternoons were devoted to poker if there were no chores to be done. The men held their places at the table and pulled out an assortment of gold coins along with wads of greenbacks. The limit, decreed by Dolan, was a dollar, with two dollars on a pair showing, check and raise allowed. He wisely kept the stakes low, to avoid either big losers or sore losers with so many men confined to one cabin. Someone produced a tattered deck of cards and the game began.

The first hand dealt was five card stud. Jordan caught a trey in the hole and another on the board. Across from him, Hall opened for a dollar with a king showing. Dolan and Grove folded, and the other men called. On the next card, Jordan caught another trey, which gave him three of a kind. When he bet two dollars, Langham and Urschel got out, and the last two players, Doc Irvin and Hall, just called. The fourth card did nothing to improve Jordan's hand, but Hall pulled a second king. He bet two dollars.

Jordan lit a fresh smoke. "Treys raise two simoleons."

Seated to his left, Irvin folded. "Too rich for my blood. Luther, you gonna keep him honest?"

"Damn right," Hall said querulously. "Your two and two more."

Jordan took the last raise. On the fifth card, neither of the men improved their hands on the board. Hall bet and Jordan again raised the limit. For a moment, Hall studied the cards, his brow furrowed. Then he looked up at Jordan.

"You're bluffin'," he said. "Cost you two more."

"Two more says I'm not bluffin'."

Hall called the raise. Jordan flipped his hole card and spread three treys. The other men watched as Hall hesitated, then angrily turned his cards facedown. Dolan chortled a dry laugh, his expression sardonic.

"Luther, you're snakebit! Looks like you can't whip Sam at anything."

Hall's eyes went smoky. "Him and me aren't through yet."

"You talking cards"—Jordan stared at him—"or something else?"

Out of the corner of his eye, Jordan saw Bascom turn from the dishpan. The other men sat perfectly still, waiting for the half-breed to reply. A long, deadened silence slipped past while Hall weighed his next move. Finally, though the challenge was obvious to everyone, he appeared to have second thoughts. He shoved his cards into the middle of the table.

"One hand ain't a game. Somebody deal."

Dolan burst out laughing. "Goddamm, Luther, wipe your mouth. You got egg on your face."

"Don't push it," Hall said coldly. "Let well enough alone."

"Luther, when I push, you'll be the first one to know. Take my word for it."

Buster Fenton collected the cards and began shuffling. The other men counted their coins, or stared off at the walls. Dolan calmly stared at Luther Hall, his eyes like glass.

Jordan figured it to be a long afternoon. And an even longer night.

# NINETEEN

**S**upper provided only a momentary interruption in the poker game. After the meal, Dolan allowed jugs of corn whiskey to be brought out. The liquor was raw and potent, produced by backwoods Cherokee in crude stills.

Dolan was a harsh and sometimes demanding leader. Yet he tempered discipline with a keen insight into the ways of rough men. During the day, he prohibited drinking and enforced the rule with an iron hand. But once the evening meal was finished, the men were free to indulge themselves. Dolan, who liked a nip himself, regularly joined them.

When the game resumed, Jordan adopted caution as his watchword. He purposely folded winning hands and made it a point to avoid another head-to-head confrontation with Hall. After washing the supper dishes, Bascom adopted a similar attitude upon taking a seat in the game. Their single goal was to recover the Durham bull and depart the hideout with no further mishap. Neither of them wanted to risk delay by chancing trouble with Hall.

Nor were they willing to risk too much corn whiskey. Their plan for later that night demanded clear heads and quick thinking. One miscue, particularly after Dolan had taken them into his confidence, would get them killed. With that in mind, they drank sparingly, pretending that the rotgut whiskey was not to their taste, which required no great acting on their part. The liquor was molten, a form of liquid fire.

The other men drank as though weaned on Cherokee mash. To all appearances their gullets were lined with steel, and they downed the whiskey as though it were aged rye. By mid-evening, none of them was feeling any pain. Some of them held it better than others, but slurred speech and nodding heads indicated the whiskey was having an effect. An hour or so later Dolan called an end to the poker game.

The men staggered off to their bunks. Some of them stripped to their long johns, while others hit the covers fully clothed. The long day and the potent whiskey quickly worked as a sedative. Within minutes, the cabin filled with the wheezy snores of men sapped by drink. Around the room, the beans they'd consumed at noontime, and again at supper, took a flatulent toll. Several of the men, deep in slumber, broke wind with the rumble of distant thunder.

Dolan was in a talkative mood. By no means drunk, his tongue was nonetheless loosened by the corn liquor. He stayed at the table with Jordan and Bascom, talking in a low voice. His remarks were those of a man who had few, if any, friends. He saw

Jordan, in particular, as a man much like himself. Tough and pragmatic, someone he could command as well as respect. There was little doubt that his agreeable manner stemmed in great part from his own interests. He saw Jordan as a likely replacement for his surly lieutenant, Luther Hall.

Among other things, they learned that Dolan was originally from Missouri. He'd come west after the Civil War, working first on the railroads and later as a cowhand in New Mexico. There, he had fallen in with bad company and eventually joined a band of rustlers operating out of No Man's Land. Before long he'd come to the conclusion that stealing horses and cows in small bunches was penny-ante stuff. The pay was too short for the risk involved.

Then, by happenstance, he'd met Doc Irvin. After seeing the magic of the hot wire, he had hatched the idea of going big time by stealing only prize stock. About the same time, the Katy railroad had finished laying track through Indian Territory. He'd set up operations in the Cherokee Nation, both for the proximity to a railhead and as a haven from the law. Over a period of time, he had recruited a gang of experienced thieves. No one, including federal marshals, had yet tumbled to the fact that they specialized in purebred livestock. He figured the operation was good for at least another year.

Bascom had known men in their cups to talk all night. With no end in sight, he finally decided to push things along. He yawned and spread his arms in a wide stretch. "Time to hit the hay," he said. "I can't hardly keep my eyes open."

"Yeah, me too," Jordan said, rising from the table. "I'm plumb bushed."

Dolan drained his drink. "We'll talk some more tomorrow. You boys get your beauty sleep."

Bascom shucked off his boots and crawled into his bunk. Jordan unstrapped his bedroll and spread it near the front wall. As he seated himself, pulling off his boots, he saw Dolan douse the coal-oil lamp. The gangleader wobbled across the room and flopped down on his own bunk. A moment later, one booted foot dangling off the bunk, he joined the chorus of snores echoing through the cabin.

Some minutes passed while Jordan lay stretched out on the bedroll. Then, pushing himself erect, he rose to his feet and collected his boots. As he moved toward the door, Bascom eased out of his bunk and snuggled his boots close to keep the spurs from jingling. He froze when Buster Fenton, who occupied the top bunk, rolled over and muttered something in a sleepy voice. After a long moment, he tiptoed across the floor in stocking feet.

Jordan gingerly slipped the latch on the door. He opened it a crack, then wider, wary of a creak from the hinges. He waited until Bascom moved past him before stepping outside. With great care, he gently closed the door and lowered the latch. He joined Bascom and they catfooted to the end of the building, where an open equipment shed was attached to the side of the cabin. Their rumps braced against the wall, they tugged on their boots.

"What d'you think?" Bascom whispered. "Are we in the clear?"

"So far," Jordan said. "Let's just hope nobody wakes up and has to drain his lizard."

"How you wanna handle this?"

"Let's get the horses saddled. Then we'll tend to the bull."

"Lord love us, never thought I'd turn rustler in my old age."

"You'd better pray we've got the gift for it. Otherwise they'll nail our hides to the wall."

"Sam, you could've said damn near anything but that."

Jordan moved into the shed. He hefted his saddle from a split-rail rack and remembered to gather a snap-link lead rope he'd spotted the day before. Bascom collected his own saddle gear and followed him outside. The clearing shimmered in bright starlight as they walked toward the stock pens. Somewhere across the river an owl hooted from the darkened woods.

The section of stock pens nearest the cabin served as a corral for the gang's horses. While Jordan stood guard, Bascom eased through the gate. His voice soft and muted, he gentled the animals as he moved around the enclosure. One at a time he slipped bridle and bit onto the roan and buckskin, and led them outside. The horses stood ground-reined as Jordan and Bascom swung first the saddle blankets and then the saddles into place. Working quickly, they snugged the cinches down tight.

Jordan led the way. They kept the stock pens between themselves and the cabin, circling around in the direction of the river. On the opposite side they halted before the Durham's corral. The bull stood at the rear of the enclosure, eyeing them with a baleful stare. He snuffed, lifting a massive hoof, and pawed the ground.

"Jesus," Bascom said softly. "You reckon that bastard's gonna come along peaceable?"

"Why not?" Jordan looked less certain than he sounded. "Hall stole him easy enough. No reason he'd give us any trouble."

"I recollect Lord Ingram sayin' he's a gentle sort. Follow you anywhere."

"All we've got to do is get that snap-link hooked on to his nose ring."

"Oh, is that all?" Bascom said in a testy whisper. "You ever hooked anything onto a bull's nose before?"

"Nope," Jordan admitted. "Never had any reason to try."

"Closest I've ever been to a full-growed bull was at the end of a rope. And that was from horseback."

"Well hell, Newt, you just said yourself that Ingram told us he's tame as a tabby-cat. Why're we stallin'?"

The bull pawed the earth. Bascom watched him with a jaundiced eye. "That dumb brute look tame to you?"

Jordan frowned. "Not just exactly."

"So who's gonna put a leash on him?"

"You always had a way with animals. I've seen you tackle lots worse than that."

"Gawdalmighty," Bascom grumped. "You're awful brave with my hide, ain't you?"

"Just keep callin' him Homer. He's likely partial to the name."

"Says you."

Bascom slipped the gate latch. He took the lead rope and stepped into the corral. The bull backed up another step, lowering his head, and pawed a shower of dirt against the fence posts. One step at a time, Bascom edged across the enclosure. His voice was low and muffled, cajoling.

"C'mon now, Homer. Just take 'er slow and easy. Nothin' to trouble yourself about."

The bull glowered at him. Bascom moved a step closer, then another, talking all the time. Finally, separated by an arm's length, Bascom stretched out his hand, the snap-link ready. Suddenly, as though lulled by the gentle voice, the bull sniffed the outstretched hand. Bascom snapped onto the nose ring.

Still cautious, Bascom lifted the lead rope, exerting the slightest tug on the nose ring. The bull plodded forward, closing the distance in two steps, and halted. Bascom stared at him in wonderment for a brief moment, then craned around to look at Jordan. His mouth split in a nutcracker grin.

"Looky there, Sam! Ol' Homer leads pretty as you please."

"So bring him on along. We haven't got all night."

"Listen to who's givin' orders. I could've got stomped into a greasy spot, for chrissake!"

"Newt, would you just haul his ass outta there?"

"C'mon, Homer," Bascom said pleasantly. "Let's show this ingrate what a good feller you are."

The bull followed after him like a docile house pet. Jordan watched them approach, preoccupied with opening the gate. His attention diverted, he failed to see a figure materialize off to his side, on the opposite side of the gate. Luther Hall's voice ripped through the night.

"What the hell you bastards up to?"

Jordan's head whipped around. He saw starlight flicker off the gun in Hall's hand. His action was one of sheer reflex, less thought than visceral instinct. He slammed the gate into Hall's arm and sent the gun spinning off into the dark. Hall yelped, staggering backward, and clutched his arm.

Jordan was on him in an instant. The first blow knocked him into the fence posts, and the second, a fist buried deep in his stomach, took his breath. Stepping back, Jordan measured him and then hammered him to the ground with a straight right to the jaw. Hall dropped with a dusty thud.

Working quickly, Jordan unbuckled the half-breed's belt and slipped it from his pants. He knelt, pulling Hall's arms to the rear, and knotted the belt tight around the wrists. Then he tore the man's shirt apart, and used one end to bind the ankles. The other end was looped through the bound arms and drawn back to the ankles in a secure knot. The end result left Luther Hall hog-tied.

Jordan added the finishing touch with a bandanna taken from Hall's hip pocket. He wrenched the half-breed's jaws open and stuffed the wadded bandanna into his mouth. Satisfied that Hall could neither move nor call out, he climbed to his feet. He looked around to find Bascom and the bull admiring his handiwork.

"Quick thinkin'," Bascom said. "Where'd the bastard come from?"

"Don't know," Jordan replied, casting a glance at the cabin. "We'd better make tracks before anybody else pops up."

"By God, I'll second that motion."

Jordan stepped into the saddle. He held the bull's lead rope while Bascom mounted. Then, with a last glance at the cabin, they turned out of the clearing.

Homer followed them west into the night.

# TWENTY

**L**uther Hall silently awaited sunrise. When he'd regained his senses, he had spent an hour or so in a futile struggle to break free. There was no doubt that he had been bound by a cowhand, someone who knew how to truss a steer, or a man. The bonds around his wrists and ankles were tight as a rawhide lariat.

Hall had finally stopped struggling. He realized there was no way to free himself and sound the alarm. Instead, like a common worm, he began wriggling on his belly toward the cabin. His progress was inch by inch, a matter of rocking back and forth on his stomach and then hurling himself forward. Sometimes the maneuver advanced him less than an inch, or not at all.

The effort required was herculean. Every rocking and hurling motion took all the strength he could muster. His idea was to somehow squirm to the cabin and rouse the crew by kicking on the door. But with each effort his energy was further sapped, and he took longer to recover. At times, he lost his balance and rolled onto his side, floundering like a landed catfish. The struggle to roll back onto his belly leached what remained of his strength.

Shortly after first light his wormlike journey ceased. He'd spent the night inching across the space separating the stock pens from the cabin. He was not within ten feet of the cabin door, but he could go no farther. His chest heaved, his breathing was ragged, and the wadded bandanna had left his mouth dry as a bone. His arms and legs were numb from the tight bonds, and his bowed spine was seared with pain. He was exhausted, his stamina spent, and he could endure no more. He lay waiting in the murky dawn.

Hall was furious with himself. He'd had the drop on Jordan and Bascom, and plain to see they were stealing the Durham bull. He should have shot them where they stood, ended it there. Instead, perhaps because he was fearful of hitting the bull, he had hesitated an instant too long. He cursed himself that he'd allowed Jordan to beat him senseless and leave him hog-tied. He felt shamed, somehow deballed, by being overpowered so easily.

Yet, however furious with himself, he was enraged with Rafe Dolan. It was Dolan who had brought the two strangers into the camp, casually forgiven them for killing Clute Johnson. Worse, Dolan had intentionally set Jordan against him, goaded them into a fight. There was no doubt that Dolan meant for Jordan to replace him, take over as second in command. The men knew it and he knew it, for Dolan had openly insulted him, held him up to contempt. He'd been betrayed and ridiculed, made to look the fool.

Hall's rage suddenly cooled before a more immediate problem. Last night he'd awakened with the urgent need to take a leak. During the course of his struggles, he had forgotten his bladder in the effort to sound an alarm. But now, exhausted and hurting, there was no denying the call of nature. His gut felt distended, ready to explode, and he knew he couldn't hold it much longer. Unless something happened damned soon, he would suffer the greatest indignity of all. He was about to piss his pants.

Streamers of sunlight flamed on the eastern horizon. Several moments later the door of the cabin opened and Buster Fenton stepped outside. He knuckled sleep from his eyes, then stretched, his mouth wide in a jaw-cracking yawn. He turned, heading toward the privy, when he caught a wriggling movement off to the side. He looked down in oxlike amazement at Hall.

"Luther—" He paused, still befuddled by whiskey and drugged with sleep. "What the hell happened to you?"

Hall grunted a muffled moan. His eyes flashed and his head jerked with a spastic urging motion. Fenton hurried forward, pulling a jackknife from his pants pocket. He bent down and snipped Hall's bonds with the blade. Arms and legs freed, Hall flopped over on his back. He raised a shaky hand, jerking the sodden bandanna from his mouth.

"Holy shit!" Fenton said, still dumbfounded. "Who done this to you, Luther?"

Hall attempted to stand. His legs gave way, and needles of fire made him wince as blood raced back into his limbs. He glanced up at Fenton.

"Get me on my feet."

Fenton moved behind him, stooped down, and lifted him off the ground. Hall's legs were wobbly, and Fenton grasped him around the chest, holding him erect. Fumbling with the buttons on his pants, Hall pulled out his pud and let go. He breathed a huge sigh of relief as a gusher of water splattered dust at his feet.

"Goddarn," Fenton said, peering over his shoulder. "You really had to piss, didn't you?"

"So bad it made my teeth hurt."

"How'd you come to get tied up like that?"

"Them two assholes," Hall said, still watering the ground. "Jordan and his sidekick."

"Bascom?" Fenton said, clearly bewildered. "Yeah, I seen he wasn't in his bunk when I got up. Figured he'd gone to the outhouse."

"He's long gone, awright. Lit out last night."

"I don't understand none of this, Luther. Why'd they hog-tie you that way?"

Hall tucked himself back into his pants. "Buster, I can't walk too good just yet. Help me into the cabin."

Fenton got an arm around his waist. Hall threw one arm over his shoulder and they hobbled toward the door. Inside, supporting most of his weight, Fenton lugged him to the table and lowered him into a chair. The room still echoed with the snores of sleeping men.

*"Dolan!"* Hall yelled. "Wake the hell up!"

The shout was like a thunderclap to men suffering a hangover. Some of them moaned and others clutched their heads, their eyes wide and bloodshot. Dolan levered himself erect, still fully clothed, and sat on the edge of the bunk. He stared at Hall with a glum expression.

"Why you yellin' so loud?"

"Not half as loud as you're gonna yell. Them two saddle-tramps you hired on took off last night."

"Sam?" Dolan asked, blinking away confusion. "Newt?"

"Yassuh, boss," Hall said with biting sarcasm. "Good ol' Sam and Newt. Done deserted the bunch."

The tone behind the words stung. Dolan stiffened, his gaze suddenly angry. "Keep your smart-ass mouth to yourself. Just tell me what you're talkin' about."

"I'm talkin' about that Durham bull. The one I trailed all the way from the Panhandle. Jordan and Bascom stole him."

"Stole him?"

Dolan parrotted the words in an incredulous voice. The other men gaped at Hall as though he'd just sprouted wildflowers from either ear. Hall was clearly amused by the reaction he'd drawn. He stared back at Dolan with a gleeful, wicked grin.

"You heard right. The bastards stole that bull slick as spit. I seen 'em with my own eyes."

"What d'you mean?" Dolan demanded. "How'd you see them?"

Hall's smile slipped a notch. "Well, I went out to

take a piss and there they was. All set to lead that
bull off."

"Why didn't you stop 'em?"

"Wasn't because I didn't try. Drew down on them
and told 'em to hold it right there."

"So what happened?"

Fenton couldn't stand it. "They got away," he
blurted. "I found Luther trussed up like a Christmas
goose. Cut him loose and he pissed a regular goddamn river. You never seen anything like it."

Dolan waved him off. "Tell me," he said to Hall.
"How'd they jump you when you had the drop on
them?"

"No, you don't!" Hall protested. "You're not
shifting the blame onto me. Wasn't me that brought
'em here and made them right to home. You're the
one to answer for that."

"I don't answer for nothin'!"

Dolan stood, surveying the men with an angry
glare. His gaze stopped on Hall. "I'm the one that
asks the questions around here. Anybody don't like
it, now's the time to speak your piece."

Hall would have accepted the offer had it involved a no-holds-barred fistfight. But he, like the
other men, knew that he was no match for Dolan
where it came to gunplay. He was all too aware as
well that the gangleader brooked no nonsense from
his men. Dolan would kill anyone who challenged
his authority.

When no one replied, Dolan stumped over and
sat down at the table. He put his head in his hands,
as though trying to collect his thoughts. At last, al-

most sadly, he looked up. "Doesn't make any sense," he said as if thinking aloud. "Why would they steal that bull?"

The men appeared equally baffled. After a time, Hall shifted in his chair. "They was penny-ante thieves," he said. "Maybe they saw a chance to strike it rich. You said it yourself, Rafe. That bull's worth a heap of money."

Dolan's eyes narrowed. "Wouldn't that take the goddamn cake. After I gave 'em a job and all—and they steal from me?"

Hall cleared his throat. "Just hope you didn't—uh, you know—tell 'em too much. Like how we unload rustled stock."

For a long moment, Dolan sat staring off into space. He knew he'd been played for a fool, conned by a couple of two-bit grifters. He thought Hall was probably right, that Jordan and Bascom had jumped at the chance for a big payday. But that lessened not at all the anger he felt, especially toward Jordan. He'd taken the son-of-a-bitch into his confidence, and trusted him. Trusted him with secrets that could destroy everything it had taken years to build.

"Last night," he said to Hall, "you see which way they went?"

"Can't say I did," Hall admitted. "Jordan cold-cocked me and I was out when they took off. Spent the rest of the night tryin' to crawl up to the cabin."

"Why didn't you yell out?"

Hall's features darkened. "They stuffed a ker-chief halfways down my throat."

"Cute pair, them two." Dolan was silent a moment. "How long a lead you figure they've got on us?"

"I'd judge maybe seven or eight hours. 'Course, there's a good chance we can cut that down real quick. You'll recollect what I told you about that bull. Bastard won't be hurried for nothin', just ambles along."

"They wouldn't have much trouble sellin' the bull, not since Doc changed his brand. Question is, where would they try?"

"You're askin' me," Hall ventured. "I'd say Wichita or Dodge. They'd try to dump him at a livestock market—quick money."

Dolan suddenly began barking orders. Doc Irvin, still in his long johns, fired up the stove and started cooking breakfast. Fenton and Grove pulled out saddlebags and gathered foodstuffs for several days on the trail. The rest of the men trooped outside to saddle horses.

Hall was assigned the job of tracker. Whether true or not, the fact that he was a half-breed led everyone to believe he was better suited to the task. Outside, he walked to the stock pen where the bull had been quartered. The glint of sunlight on metal caught his eye and he recovered his pistol. Then, taking a position beside the corral gate, he studied the ground. The earth was still moist from the night's dew, and the tracks were easy to read. He followed them across the clearing and a short distance into the woods. The direction was due west.

Upon returning to the cabin, he explained the sign to Dolan. What he'd said earlier, about Wichita or Dodge, seemed even more likely. At some point, he observed, Jordan and Bascom would bear off north by northwest. Dolan accepted the news without comment.

After breakfast, Irvin and Urschel were ordered to stay behind and look after the livestock. Neither of them offered any complaint, for they knew the chase would be hard on man and horse alike. Dolan led the rest of the gang outside.

Mounted, they rode west, with Hall in the lead. Dolan thought the odds were just about right with five men. Five to two. Two dead men, once they were caught.

# TWENTY-ONE

The term "bull-headed" quickly took on new meaning for Jordan and Bascom. Homer disdained strenuous activity, and much preferred to travel at a sedate pace. In fact, heedless of their efforts, he refused to travel any other way.

They first tried leading him at a slow trot. When that failed, they attempted a fast walk. Then they tried chousing him, switching his butt with a lariat. Their last idea, prodding him from the rear with a stiff pole, produced equally unspectacular results. Homer's response to their every effort was exactly the same. He stopped.

Homer clearly thought of himself as a lover, not a fighter. He had been raised to breed cows, and quite obviously, he considered that to be his sole purpose in life. He took an indignant attitude toward the switching and prodding, casting a baleful eye at his tormentors. Yet he was a gentleman, albeit a stubborn one, and he refused to acknowledge the harassment by responding in kind. Instead, he retaliated with a more civilized stratagem. He simply stopped in his tracks.

Their first night on the trail, Jordan and Bascom had grown increasingly frustrated. Nothing they tried had worked, and it soon became apparent that Homer would not be rushed. He stopped, planting his massive frame in place, and refused to budge despite their vigorous tugging and prodding. He adopted a stoic manner, almost as though he held them and their brute tactics in utter contempt. They were reduced to cajoling, sometimes begging, and finally a grudging acceptance of Homer's attitude toward overland travel.

There was no question that they would be pursued by Dolan and his gang. At best, they figured they had a head start of no more than eight hours. Their first objective was to intersect the Arkansas River, roughly some twenty miles west of the gang's hideout. After several abortive attempts at hustling Homer along, they settled down to a steady walk. But it was a forced march, never pausing to rest, with one goal in mind. They had to reach the river by daylight.

Sunrise found them on the banks of the Arkansas. They reined their horses to a halt, staring westward along the river. Homer stopped behind them, his lead rope hanging slack, and began cropping the grass. The stream, at full summer, was shallow and bottomed with rocks visible through the clear water. For a time, they sat studying the rolling terrain on either side of the river. Bascom finally broke the silence.

"Got no choice," he said. "We gotta stop long enough for the animals to rest up and graze awhile. Push 'em too hard and they'll give out on us."

Jordan rolled himself a smoke. He lit up and took a long drag. "Four hours is about all we can afford. That'll cut our lead just about in half."

"Or less," Bascom said darkly. "I doubt Dolan and his boys will have any trouble followin' our trail."

"You talkin' about Luther Hall?"

"Well, he's part Injun, ain't he? Never yet saw one that wasn't a pretty fair tracker. I figger he'll keep his nose to the ground."

"Yeah, likely so." Jordan smoked in silence a moment. "Got any tricks to throw him off the scent?"

"Tell you one thing," Bascom grumped. "It's a mortal goddamm shame we can't make that bull move any faster." He turned in the saddle and glowered at Homer. "Sorry sonovabitch can't hold a candle to a longhorn. Way he hitches along, you'd think his legs was broke."

"Careful what names you call him. He's liable to sull up and not move at all."

"Swear to Christ, I've seen mules that was more agreeable. Bastard acts like he's royalty or some such."

Jordan nodded. "We know now why it took Hall so long to get back from the Panhandle. Homer wouldn't shade a turtle by a whole helluva lot."

"Amen to that," Bascom said. "Way I calculate it, we're better'n two hundred fifty miles from home ground. 'Course, that's as the crow flies—and Homer ain't no crow."

"The rate we're travelin'"—Jordan did some quick figuring—"that's close to a couple of weeks on the trail."

"Not to mention we could have company the whole goldarned way. Dolan and that half-breed are gonna stick to us like fleas on a dog."

"Are you saying there's no way to ditch them?"

"Nooo," Bascom allowed, with a thoughtful frown. "I've still got some tricks up my sleeve."

"Like what?"

"Just for openers, we'll try swimmin' upstream."

"Come again?"

"Take a look." Bascom gestured at the river. "Water's real shallow this time of year. We're gonna wade right up the middle."

Jordan puffed his cigarette, exhaled smoke on a faint breeze. "You think that'll fool Hall?"

"Hard to follow tracks in a riverbed. Not that it can't be done, you understand. Just takes a lot longer."

"Yeah, but it'll slow us down, too. No way we'll make good time in the water."

"Well, pardner, it's not like we've got a helluva lot of choice. If we stick to land, we're gonna leave sign. Dolan would run us down like he had a compass up his ass."

Jordan flipped his cigarette into the water. "You'll recollect the Arkansas angles off to the northwest. The Panhandle's due west of here."

"We'll follow it till it connects with the Cimarron. Then we'll follow that till it crosses the Chisholm Trail."

"And then what?"

Bascom grinned. "I reckon I'll have to come up with a new dodge. Something that 'breed Injun ain't never heard of."

"Yeah?" Jordan said. "Such as what?"

"I'll let you know when I think of it."

They camped along the riverbank. Breakfast was scrounged from their saddlebags, hardtack and a pot of Arbuckle's coffee. Homer and the horses munched grass, and afterwards, like the men, caught up on their sleep. Later, as the sun edged toward its zenith, they broke camp.

Strung out in single file, they took to the water and rode upstream. Homer ambled along at the rear, content with the slow pace.


At sundown, five days later, they hit the Chisholm Trail. The land was open prairie, lush with grass and watered by the Cimarron. Off in the distance, a herd of some two thousand longhorns were being held for the night. A campfire winked in the approaching darkness.

Jordan and Bascom rode into the camp as stars glittered to life in an indigo sky. The chuck wagon was positioned in the center of the camp, with the wagon tongue pointed toward the North Star. Several cowhands were gathered around the fire, eating supper from tin plates. A slim, rawboned man in his late thirties set his plate on the ground and walked forward. He nodded as they brought their horses to a halt.

"Howdy," he said. "You boys lose your way?"

"Matter of fact," Jordan replied, "we're dead on the mark. Leastways if this here's the Chisholm Trail."

"Six days a week and all day on Sunday. I'm Joe Webb, trail boss for the outfit."

"Glad to make your acquaintance. I'm Sam Jordan and this here's my partner, Newt Bascom."

Jordan and Bascom were careful to observe range etiquette. A strange rider never dismounted until invited to do so by the man in charge. They waited while Webb slowly inspected them and their gear. After a moment, he stepped aside for a better look at their bull.

"What kinda critter is that, anyway?"

"Durham," Bascom informed him. "Imported all the way from England."

"That a fact?"

Webb followed the same rules of etiquette. Among cattlemen, it was considered impolite to ask direct questions. Where they were headed, and why they were leading a Durham bull through the wilderness, was their business. Unless they volunteered the information, no one would ask. Webb finally nodded.

"Whyn't you boys stake that critter out and unsaddle your ponies. You're welcome to supper."

"Thank you kindly," Jordan said. "We won't be a minute."

After borrowing rope and a stake, they found Homer a grassy spot within sight of the camp. They then unsaddled and turned their horses in with the outfit's remuda. The cowhands nodded greeting as they approached the fire, and the cook brought them plates of stew, spotted-dog rice, and Dutch-oven biscuits. They polished it off with considerable gusto, gratefully accepting steaming mugs of coffee. Webb shook his head as they set their plates aside.

"You boys act like you haven't et in a while."

"Not real cookin'," Bascom admitted. "We've been on the trail for nearabout a week."

Jordan rolled himself a smoke. "We're playin' nursemaid to that bull." He took a smoldering stick from the fire, lit his cigarette. "Owner hired us to take him down the trail."

Webb tried to sound casual. "Would I know the outfit?"

Nothing would be served by trying to explain who they were or how they came to be there. Jordan decided instead to shade the truth. "The Lazy L," he said. "Out west of Fort Worth."

"Wouldn't know 'em," Webb commented. "We're Broken Arrow H, down around San Antone." He motioned off into the darkness. "Why'd anybody want a bull like that 'un?"

"Mostly for breeding," Bascom said. "Hefty feller like that puts lots of meat on his offspring. Better beeves fetch higher prices."

Webb looked amused. "Gawd, wouldn't that be a sight! Can't you see it, that big scutter toppin' a mama longhorn. Probably drive her into the ground up to her hocks."

The cowhands seated around the fire nodded and chuckled. Bascom started to laugh, then abruptly turned sober. The expression on his face was that of a man who had suddenly seen a riddle solved at last. He stared across the fire at Webb.

"What you just said gave me an idea. Wonder if you'd be willin' to sell us a cow?"

Webb appeared confused. "Why'd you want a cow?"

Jordan was no less curious. Bascom gestured off at the staked-out Durham. "That bull's an ornery cuss," he said. "Won't make no speed a'tall on the trail. Figgered it'd put a little spring in his step if he had himself a lady friend."

"See your point," Webb said. "Put a cow out front of him and that'll just naturally jitterate his juices. That the idea?"

"Shore wouldn't slow him down none."

"You know, I got just the thing. A heifer got mixed in with our bunch, and nobody noticed till we was up the trail. She likely wouldn't fetch nothin' at railhead."

"A heifer!" Bascom said, grinning. "Let him follow some young stuff and he'd step right out. How much you want for her?"

"Ten dollars sound fair?"

"You just made yourself a deal."

Later, when they were bedded down for the night, Jordan chuckled softly. "Homer's gonna think you hung the moon. Been a long time since he sniffed a female."

"Hope to hell it works," Bascom muttered. "We gotta travel cross-country from here to the Canadian. I'd like to get it done before we lose our lead."

"You think Dolan's still on our trail?"

"All depends on that half-breed. If he's as good a tracker as I am, then I'd doubt we've lost him. Just a matter of how much we slowed him down."

Jordan considered a moment. "When he hits the Chisholm, won't that throw him off? There must be a million tracks along here."

"Yeah, it might," Bascom said. "'Course, I always follow the lesson we learned when we was fightin' blue-bellies, back during the war. Don't never underestimate your enemy."

"When we started out on this job, Hall lost us easy enough on Red Deer Creek. Guess we have to assume he knows his business."

"Not to mention the fact that he's plumb loco to skin your hide."

"Dolan's probably already got dibs on me, don't you think?"

"I just suspect he hates you worse'n the devil hates holy water."

Jordan thought that summed it up in a nutshell. Rafe Dolan would join hands with God or the Devil if it served his purpose. His purpose now was to hunt them down.

# TWENTY-TWO

**H**omer was beguiled. The heifer was young and brindle-colored, not quite two years old. She seemed to sense that the bull was smitten by her charms. She playfully teased him, presenting her round hind end, and staring back over her shoulder with liquid brown eyes. Homer trundled after her like a lovesick suitor.

Jordan rode out front. A rope was dallied around his saddle horn and the other end was affixed to the heifer's neck. He set the pace at something between a fast walk and a half-trot. Bascom brought up the rear, with the bull hooked by the nose to the lead rope. Homer's fondness for leisurely travel was now a thing of the past. His eye on the heifer, he matched the horses stride for stride.

On a straight line, the stretch of prairie between the Chisholm Trail and the Canadian River was roughly forty miles. The ground-eating pace set by Jordan greatly increased their rate of travel. Upon departing the cow camp, they had set a course south by southwest. The country was open and fairly level, which allowed them to take a bearing as the crow flies. Homer, after his first look at the heifer, never once attempted to slow their progress. He went from laggard to fast-stepper in the blink of an eye.

Late the second afternoon, they spotted the Canadian. The river curved and twisted on a westerly course through scattered timber. Far off in the distance a range of low hills stood silhouetted against the horizon. Beyond the hills was the demarcation line between Indian Territory and the Texas Panhandle.

Jordan halted at the edge of the riverbank. Bascom stopped a short distance downstream, far enough to keep the bull and the heifer separated. Homer's tongue lolled out and he was breathing heavily from the steady pace. For the moment he was more interested in water than the witchery of his young traveling companion. The animals lowered their heads and swilled from the stream.

"Gotta hand it to you," Jordan said. "That heifer was a stroke of genius. She's sure done a trick on Homer."

Bascom grunted. "Got him thinkin' with his balls instead of his brains. He'd follow that little girl till he dropped."

"Well, we don't want to risk that. We have to get him back to Lord Ingram in good shape."

"Way we're hot-footin' it along, he's gonna shed weight. He ain't built for speed."

Jordan eased forward in his saddle, gave the bull a closer look. "Maybe we ought to slow down some. Hate to come this far and have him fall down dead."

Bascom studied the angle of the sun. "We'll make camp in another hour or so. Once he gets a bellyful of grass, he'll perk up right smart."

"Still think we'd better slow down. He's lookin' a mite tuckered out."

"Not half as bad as we'll look if Dolan catches up. You more worried about that bull, or yourself?"

Jordan took out the makings. He built a cigarette and lit it with a match. After taking a drag, he dropped the match on the riverbank. "We're bustin' our butts," he said, "and maybe it's all for nothing. We could've lost Dolan days ago."

"Yeah, we could've," Bascom said with no great conviction. "But I'd sooner operate on the theory that he ain't far behind. The other way round could get us killed." He paused, squirted the ground with a shot of tobacco juice. "Get ourselves killed, we'll lose Homer in the bargain. Don't forget that."

A time passed as Jordan stared off at the distant hills. He took a long, slow pull on his cigarette, then exhaled. "I'd put us about a hundred miles out from the Circle I. You agree?"

"Give or take a few miles. Why d'you ask?"

"The way we've been humpin' along, we'd make it there in about five days. Or we could rest Homer a spell and take our time. Day or so wouldn't matter one way or another."

"No, it wouldn't." Bascom jerked his head to the rear. "Not unless Dolan's hot on our trail."

Jordan smiled. "Pardner, maybe I've got more faith in you than you've got in yourself. After all the tricks you pulled, how could anybody still be doggin' us?" He tapped an ash off his cigarette. "Take a goddamn bloodhound to turn up sign back there at the Chisholm."

"Let's suppose I'm Luther Hall. You know how I'd go about it?"

"How?"

"First off, I'd figger you probably headed for Wichita. That'd be the place to sell a prize bull real quick for top dollar. 'Course, there's no way I could be plumb certain you headed north, is there?"

"No, I reckon not. Too many tracks on the Chisholm for a clear read."

"That's a fact," Bascom affirmed. "So before I galloped off to Wichita, I'd nose around here and there. Just to make sure you hadn't pulled another swift one."

Jordan looked unconvinced. "Like what?"

"Like making a beeline cross-country for the Western Trail. Which leads to Dodge City."

"The direction we're headed right now?"

"Yep," Bascom said tersely. "I might figger you'd figger I wouldn't think you'd head for Dodge. So I'd ride circles west of the Chisholm, just to play it safe. Try to cut sign."

Jordan was thoughtful now. "And you'd find our trail . . ."

"Any tracker worth his salt would find it. No way in hell to hide two horses and a bull. Not to mention the heifer."

There was a long moment of deliberation. At length, Jordan nodded his head. "Guess you've got a point. But why keep runnin' unless you're right? Why not check it out?"

Bascom cocked one eye. "How you figger to do that?"

"Well—" Jordan motioned the way they'd come. "If Hall's part bloodhound, he wouldn't have any trouble trackin' us across flat ground. Probably do it at a lope and still not lose the trail. Hell, he could be on our heels any minute now."

Bascom stared back over the wide prairie. Then he gave Jordan a suspicious look. "You've hatched some harebrained scheme, haven't you?"

Jordan dug the small brass telescope out of his saddlebags. "I'll wait here," he said. "If they show up before sundown, I'll be able to spot them a mile or so away. If they don't show, then we're in the clear."

"What am I supposed to be doing all this time?"

"You take Homer and his lady friend and head upstream. I'll follow along before full dark."

"Hold on," Bascom objected. "How am I gonna lead Homer and the heifer at the same time? He'll climb all over her."

"Likely try it," Jordan said. "'Course, after she kicks his jaw out of socket a couple of times, he'll get the message. He's big, but he's no dummy."

"How about you?"

"What about me?"

"I know how your mind works. You're dummy enough to try and slow 'em down if they was to show up. Throw a little lead their way and give me time to get clear. That the idea?"

Jordan averted his gaze. "C'mon now, Newt. You think I'd do a fool thing like that?"

"Damn bet'cha!" Bascom said hotly. "It'd be just like you!"

"So where's that leave us?"

"Only one way I'll head upstream. I gotta have your word you won't try no nonsense. Otherwise I stay put."

"Awright," Jordan conceded. "You've got my word."

"On your oath?"

"Yeah, for chrissake! On my oath."

"You let me down and I won't never forgive you."

"You're wastin' time, Newt. Get a move on."

Bascom took the heifer's lead rope. With a final nod, he led Homer and the young longhorn into the river. Jordan dismounted and took a position in the trees bordering the shoreline. He watched, smiling to himself, as Homer tried nosing the heifer's rump and got a sharp kick in the mouth for his efforts. He heard Bascom swear at them, and a moment later, they disappeared around the bend upstream. He found a comfortable spot at the base of a large cottonwood.

Silence descended over the treeline. Except for the ripple of the water, and leaves rustling in a faint breeze, there was neither movement nor sound. He leaned back against the cottonwood, legs crossed at the ankles, and stared out across the prairie. Unbidden, a lonesome feeling crept over him. He suddenly realized that this was the first time in weeks he'd been separated from Bascom. Then, laughing at himself, he shook the feeling off.

The sun dropped lower against the distant hills. Jordan's eyelids drooped, and he caught himself on the verge of nodding off. He was worn out, tired from too little sleep and too many days on the trail. Hauling a stubborn bull along, constantly looking over his shoulder, had cost him more than he'd realized. Fearful of dozing off, he pushed himself erect and stamped his feet on the ground. The roan gelding gave him a wall-eyed look and went back to cropping the sparse grass beneath the trees. He pulled out the makings.

After sprinkling tobacco into the paper, he stuffed the bag into his pocket. He rolled the cigarette and brought it up to lick the paper. Then, suddenly, he froze with the cigarette pressed to his mouth. A slight movement, far off in the distance, had caught his eye. Heat waves, or the angle of the sun, sometimes caused distortion of light on open plains. A man often thought he'd seen movement when actually it was a trick of nature. But a closer look convinced him that his eyes weren't lying.

The cigarette fluttered from his fingers. He stepped behind the cottonwood and pulled out the telescope. One hand on the tree, forming a steady platform, he brought the telescope to his eye. He held it there, staring intently through the lens, focused on blurred movement that was too distant for clarity. Several minutes passed, and slowly, as a mirage might coalesce into reality, the shimmering movement assumed shape and form. The larger forms, the horses, gradually came into focus. A moment later the small indistinct shapes were transformed into men.

There were five riders. They came on at a steady lope, with one a short distance out front of the others. His eye glued to the telescope, Jordan had no doubt that the lead rider was Luther Hall. Details were still unclear, and they hadn't yet moved close enough to make out their features. But there was no question in his mind that the second rider in the string would be Rafe Dolan. The identity of the others was unimportant, a matter of no great consequence. What counted was that the riders were on a straight line, following tracks that led to the spot where he stood. He slowly collapsed the telescope.

Turning from the treeline, he walked to his horse. As he started to mount, his eye went to the rifle in his saddle-scabbard. He thought it would be simple to take a position behind the cottonwood, wait until the riders were within a couple of hundred yards, and open fire. At worst, he would kill some of their horses and force the others to scatter. He could easily hold them off until dark, perhaps killing a few in the bargain, and then slip away. But as his hand touched the rifle-stock, he remembered that he'd given his word. An oath extracted on the basis of trust.

The riders were drawing closer. He stepped into the saddle and reined the gelding down the riverbank. Screened by the trees, he kept the roan to midstream until he was out of sight beyond the distant bend. Farther west, the sun settled below the hills in a splash of orange and gold. He nudged the gelding into a fast trot, reining him onto the shoreline. The light slowly faded into dusk.

An hour later Newt Bascom stepped out from behind a tree. Dark had fallen and starlight glittered off the rifle he held in his hands. Jordan reined his horse to a halt and climbed down out of the saddle. Bascom spit, wiping his mustache, and grinned.

"Seen it for yourself, did you?"

Jordan nodded. "Counted five of them. They'll likely camp back where we stopped this afternoon."

"Likely so," Bascom said. " 'Course, come daylight, they'll spot our tracks. We've got no lead a'-tall now."

"Where's Homer and the heifer?"

"Got 'em picketed over in the trees. Big bastard's moony as a lovesick goose."

"Better happy and dumb than worryin' about Dolan."

"So what's your thoughts on tomorrow?"

"Figured we'd hide and watch, see what happens."

"And if that don't work?"

"Well then, Newt, I've got first crack at Rafe Dolan."

# TWENTY-THREE

**F**alse dawn brought a smudged light to the sky. Jordan and Bascom had made a cold camp overnight, wary of revealing their position with a fire. Their breakfast was short and hurried, dried fruit, hardtack and water. They were saddled and on the move as the sky paled on the eastern horizon.

There was no way to avoid leaving tracks as they led Homer and the longhorn heifer down the river-bank. The Canadian was shallow, the bottom rock-studded and firm underfoot. Bascom skirted the occasional sinkhole and sandy patches that might be disturbed by the animals' hooves. Single file, with Bascom in the lead, they rode upstream.

Not quite an hour later Bascom signaled a halt. Off to their left, a small creek fed into the stream. They had talked it over during the night, agreeing that their best chance was to try an evasive maneuver. The creek was some six feet wide, with trees lining the banks on both sides. The bottom appeared sandy, and would be easily disturbed by the hooves of four animals. But there was no great choice in the matter.

"We gotta try it," Bascom said. "God knows how far till we hit another creek."

Jordan turned in the saddle. Far behind, sunrise flooded the sky with brilliant shafts of light. "We're about out of time," he remarked. "Have to assume they broke camp at first light."

"They'd move faster, too. With five men, Dolan could cover both banks, lookin' for tracks. Don't take a half-breed to see where we came outta the water."

"You think Hall will tumble to what we've done?"

"Maybe," Bascom said. "He used the same dodge on us at Red Deer Creek. 'Course, I've got a few tricks he likely ain't seen."

They led the animals into the mouth of the creek. The bottom was soft and spongy, and silt drifted to the surface as sharp hooves displaced the muddy soil. A hundred yards upstream they found a level spot along the bank and moved onto dry land. The wooded area was far enough from the river that there was small chance of their mounts scenting the horses of Dolan's gang. A whickering snort from the roan or the buckskin would instantly betray their presence.

Working quickly, they picketed the horses in a stand of timber. Homer's lead rope was snubbed tight to a stout tree, and the heifer was tied to another tree within sniffing distance. Then, after collecting their rifles and extra cartridges, they hurried back along the shoreline. A short time later they paused some five yards from the mouth of the creek. Jordan took a position where he was hidden by the treeline and dense undergrowth. From his vantage point, he had a clear field of fire downstream.

Bascom left his rifle on the bank. He then lowered himself into the water and waded toward the mouth of the creek. Along the shore were dead trees that had rotted at the stump and fallen to the ground. With considerable effort, careful to disturb none of the nearby vegetation, he lifted several smaller trees and slanted them downward into the water. When he finished, the trees looked as though they had rotted out and toppled down the banks. The mouth of the creek was closed off by an irregular latticework of dead timber.

Gathering his rifle, Bascom joined Jordan on the shore. "Hope it works," he said. "Done my best with what was at hand."

"It'd damn sure fool me."

"Question is, will it fool that half-breed?"

"Let's suppose it don't," Jordan said. "Anybody looks cross-eyed in our direction, you drill Hall and I'll get Dolan. First come, first serve on the others."

"Won't have long to wait," Bascom said, his voice lowered to a whisper. "Here they come."

Downstream, Luther Hall rode into view. He was on the opposite bank of the river, his eyes sweeping the ground ahead along the shoreline. A moment later Dolan emerged through the scattered trees on the south bank. Strung out behind him were Buster Fenton and Jack Langham. Arnie Grove, on the other shore, trailed to the rear of Hall.

When the range closed to fifty yards, Jordan quietly earred back the hammer on his rifle. Bascom was a beat behind, the muffled click of the hammer deadly loud in the silence. Neither of them had any doubt about the effect of their .44–.40 Winchesters at close range. The slugs would down a horse, or a man, with a single shot. Jordan centered his sights on Rafe Dolan's chest. At his side, Bascom drew a bead on Hall.

The gang shortly rode abreast of the creek. Hall silently motioned them to a halt. A long moment elapsed as he sat staring across the river at the trees blocking entrance to the feeder stream. His eyes slowly inspected the irregular pattern of the fallen trees, searching for anything not put there by nature itself. At length, he signaled to Dolan, who was directly across the river. He pointed to the fallen trees.

"Have a look," he called out. "See if anything's funny about them trees dropped over the creek."

Dolan reined his horse off the shore into the river. He rode forward and halted at the mouth of the creek. Hidden in the treeline, Jordan kept his rifle sights trained on the gangleader. Bascom meanwhile had dead aim on Hall, who was watching from across the river. Dolan stared at the fallen trees for a time, then shook his head. He turned back to Hall.

"Bunch of dead trees," he said. "Broke off at the stump and slid down into the water."

"What about the banks?" Hall asked. "They could've circled around them trees. See any tracks?"

Dolan scanned the ground along both banks. His inspection was limited to the immediate shoreline

along either side of the creek. The earth was un-
marked, no rocks dislodged and no sign of hooved
animals having passed that way. He motioned to Hall.

"Nothin' out of kilter over here."

"Let's push on, then. The bastards can't be too far
ahead. They're still stickin' to the middle of the
river."

"Speed it up," Dolan ordered. "I'd like to catch
'em before sundown."

"Don't worry, we're right on their tails."

"Yeah, that's what you said last night."

Hall grunted something unintelligible. He booted
his horse in the ribs and rode west along the shoreline. Dolan swung past the creek, then nudged his
mount out of the water onto the far bank. Behind, on
either side of the river, the rest of the men followed
in single file. They rode off upstream.

When they were some distance away, Jordan
eased out from behind a tree. He glanced at Bascom,
who was still staring at the departing gang. "We
fooled them," he said. "Those trees did the trick."

"Lucky for us it was Dolan on this side of the river.
That half-breed might've taken a closer gander."

"Appears it worked out awright. What say we
make tracks out of here?"

"Hallelujah to that!" Bascom laughed. "We'll
swing south aways and then turn west overland. Be a
pleasure to quit wadin' that damn river."

"No argument there, pardner."

Ten minutes later they rode south, generally following the creek. For the first time since early that
morning, Jordan pulled out his sack of Bull Durham.

He hadn't dared light up, for fear the wind would carry the scent of smoke downstream. But now, with the gang suckered off the trail, he rolled himself a cigarette.

He savored the first puff with a long, deep drag.

Toward mid-morning, Luther Hall signaled a halt. The river had slowly emerged from timberland onto a broad plain. He sat for a moment staring off into the distance. Farther away, a low line of hills marched like sentinels on a line northward. To the direct front, on the grassy prairie, there was nothing in sight.

"What's wrong?" Dolan called from the opposite bank. "Why'd you stop?"

"Look for yourself," Hall told him. "You see anything out there?"

Dolan peered out across the prairie. "Nothin'," he said. "What am I supposed to be lookin' for?"

"Jordan and Bascom," Hall yelled out. "No way possible they outrun us that far. They'd have to be somewheres between here and that next stretch of woods."

"So where the hell are they?"

"They give us the slip somehow. Gotta be back the way we came."

Dolan's features mottled with anger. "You're supposed to be the big chief Injun tracker! How the goddamm hell'd you lose 'em?"

Hall flushed at the insult. For a moment, he sat wondering where he'd gone wrong. Not once, since they'd begun the hunt at dawn, had tracks emerged from the river. Then, struck by a sudden thought, he turned in the saddle and stared toward the rear. His mind went back to a creek, with trees toppled over in the water. The only creek they had seen all morning.

"Sonsabitches!" he cursed loudly. "They got me with my own trick!"

"What trick?" Dolan demanded. "What the shit you talkin' about?"

"That creek with the downed trees. The one you said there wasn't no sign."

"Not a lick of sign! You think I wouldn't've spotted it?"

"Yeah, I think that's just what happened."

Hall pulled his horse around with a vicious jerk on the reins. He gigged hard with his spurs and rode off downriver at a lope. Dolan hesitated a moment, taken by surprise, then hauled his horse around and rode back along the opposite bank. Fenton and Langham waited until he went past, and rammed the spurs to their mounts. Grove fell in a short distance behind Hall.

Not quite an hour later they sighted the creek. Hall put his horse down the north bank and splashed across the river. He waved off Dolan and the others. "Stay back!" he barked. "Nobody messes up the sign till I've had a look."

Hall jumped off his horse and handed the reins to Fenton. He waded into the river and moved forward until he was standing directly before the mouth of the creek. He slowly scrutinized each bank, his eyes pausing on stones and sticks and patches of vegetation. His gaze drifted past a leafy bush, then stopped and abruptly swept back. He stared intently at one of the lower branches, the stem broken and the leaves touching the ground. Dried sap, not more than a few hours old, was hardening beneath the late morning sun. He grunted softly to himself.

Wading forward, he stopped where the creek emptied into the river. The water was clear, less than two feet deep, and the muddy bottom was visible in bright sunlight. He stooped down for a closer look, and a muscle suddenly twitched along his jawline. There, in the creekbed, he saw broad holes, slowly filling with sludge brought downstream by the current. The depth of the holes, scattered in a quilt-work across the breadth of the stream, told him that several animals had been taken upstream. One of them, he knew beyond doubt, was a Durham bull.

"Gotta hand it to 'em," he said, turning to look at Dolan. "They crisscrossed them trees into the water real neat and careful. Not surprised you missed it."

Dolan kneed his horse closer. "You're sure about that, are you, Luther?"

"Double damn certain. You see that broken branch there? They clipped it when they lifted the tree down the bank. Look real close and you'll see rotted leaves on the ground dried out from the sun. Them leaves was under the dead trees."

Hall scrambled up the far bank and began searching in the timberline. Directly he stopped, staring down at bootprints in a stand of trees. His mouth tightened in a razor line. "Dirty bastards," he rumbled. "They was fixin' to bushwhack us if we caught on. Here's where they stood."

Dolan thought how very close he'd been to death. From where he had stopped at the creek, the distance to the trees was almost point-blank range. They could have blasted him off his horse with a pull of the trigger.

The bull suddenly no longer mattered. There was now a personal score to be settled.

# TWENTY-FOUR

Be good to get home."

"Damned if it won't," Bascom agreed. "What's the first thing you'll do?"

"Dump Homer," Jordan said. "Sooner we get him off our hands, the better I'll like it."

"Why hell, Sam, I thought you'd taken a shine to Homer."

"That'll be the day!"

"What's the matter?" Bascom asked, watching as Homer ambled along after the heifer. "Homer ain't hardly been no trouble a'tall."

"No trouble!" Jordan hooted. "We had people try to shoot us and a couple of knock-down-drag-out brawls. What would you call that?"

"Well, you purely enjoy fisticuffs. So that don't exactly count. As for the other, that's just business. Comes with the job."

"Listen to yourself talk. You've been bitchin' about this job since we started. Who was it that like to wet his drawers when we rode into the Nations?"

Bascom looked offended. "That ain't fair, Sam.

Anybody with a speck of sense wouldn't rest easy in the Nations. Leastways not a white man."

"An honest white man," Jordan corrected him. "Thieves and such have got themselves a good thing. Till we showed up, Dolan didn't have a worry in the world."

"Damned if that ain't the truth! Bastard was gettin' filthy rich."

They were nearing the headwater of the creek. Somewhere to the south lay the Washita River, which took a westerly course into the Panhandle. With four animals that needed daily watering, they had to stay relatively near a stream. Yet they were unfamiliar with the western reaches of Indian Territory, and the distance to the Washita was unknown. They had to make a decision.

"Creek's about petered out," Jordan noted. "Probably feeds out of an underground spring."

Bascom frowned. "Wish't I knew more about this country. The Washita's down there somewheres, no doubt of that. Just don't know how far."

"Might be too far." Jordan shaded his eyes, studied the angle of the sun. "Got four, maybe five hours of daylight left. Try it now and we're liable not to hit it before dark. We'd have to make a dry camp."

"Homer wouldn't like that. Think he was a duck, the way he takes to water."

"We could camp along here for the night. Pull out by sunrise and we're sure to strike the Washita tomorrow sometime."

Bascom nodded, thinking it over. Jordan creased a paper, filled it with tobacco, and rolled himself a cigarette. He lit up, exhaled smoke, and watched it drift away on a southerly breeze. Finally, when the silence became prolonged, he glanced around at Bascom.

"What're you thinkin' about so hard?"

"Injuns."

"You talkin' about Luther Hall?"

"Him, too," Bascom said. "But it just come to me we ain't in the Nations no more. We're in hostile territory."

Jordan wagged his head. "Wouldn't exactly call 'em hostiles. The Comanche have been on the reservation nearly two years."

"Not just the Comanche. There's Kiowa and Cheyenne and a bunch of other tribes. Way I hear it they ain't been tamed yet."

"You pullin' my leg?"

"Nope," Bascom said soberly. "Heard about some gold prospectors that disappeared in here. Rode in and never rode out."

"C'mon, Newt," Jordan said dubiously. "What makes you think they got their hair lifted?"

"Hostiles don't change that quick. Hundred years or more, this here's been their land. Like as not, they still look at intruders as fair game. 'Specially if they caught you off in the middle of nowheres."

"You're plumb nervy today, aren't you?"

"Injuns ain't the only thing on my mind. I've been thinkin' about Dolan, too."

"What about him?"

"Just suppose," Bascom said, "that we only

fooled 'em halfway. Suppose they wised up somehow and doubled back to the creek?"

Jordan smiled, puffed his cigarette. "Suppose till
you're blue in the face and that don't make it so.
They're probably halfway to New Mexico by now."

"What if they ain't?" Bascom countered. "What
if we make an early camp and they come ridin' up
the creek? We'd be in a helluva fix."

"Guess we would," Jordan conceded. "What're
you gettin' at, Newt? You want to make a run for the
Washita?"

"No, I'm not sayin' that. Just figgered I'd scout
our back trail and have a look-see. Never hurts to
play it safe."

"Go ahead, if it makes you feel any easier. I'll
keep moving along with Homer and his girlfriend.
When I find a likely spot to camp, I'll stop there."

"Shouldn't take too long. I'll catch up with you
soon's I can."

"Still think your mama raised a worrywart.
Funny thing about it, I set more stock in you than
you set in yourself. That stunt you pulled back at the
river would've thrown anybody off."

"Like I said, never underestimate your enemy."

Jordan accepted the bull's lead rope. He watched,
shaking his head in amusement, as Bascom rode
off downstream. He sometimes thought his partner
was too cautious. Then, at other times, he got
proved wrong. So maybe there was something to
the shopworn phrase after all. Never hurts to play
it safe.

. . .

Some two miles downstream Bascom halted in a stand of trees. He tied the buckskin to a thick branch and slipped his rifle from the saddle-scabbard. For a moment, he stood listening to the sounds of the woods, alert to anything unnatural. Then, satisfied that all was in order, he moved off through the timber.

The wilderness was Bascom's element. To attempt polite conversation with a respectable woman left him tongue-tied and fidgety. Even towns, which he could only take in small doses, threw him off stride. But on the plains, or in the shadowed forest, he was comfortable with himself and his surroundings. There was order and reason in nature that he rarely found in civilized society. Everything had its place and its purpose, and there were no surprises. The wilderness and its creatures operated by rules that were constant, almost immutable. A man could depend on them to do the right thing, at the right time.

Bascom ghosted through the woods. His passage was silent, disturbing nothing, leaving no trace. He was like a shadow, with no presence or form, there one moment and gone the next. When he stopped, still as the trunk of a stout oak tree, he seemed to vanish into all that was around him. He became part of the silence, what others never heard or seldom saw, because he'd learned to submerge himself into the forest. He was quiet as a cat and no less visible than a wraith. He moved without substance or sound, like smoke.

Deep within the timber, a hundred yards or more from the creek, he suddenly went still. Far downstream his eye was drawn to the glint of sun on metal. Then, off in the distance, a bluejay sent up a scolding cry, echoing through the woods. He waited, certain the glint of metal was from saddle rigging or a horse's bit, something man-made.

Finally, at least a quarter-mile downstream, he saw movement. Through the heavy timber the movement gradually took shape, a man on a horse. Then another and another, until there were five in all. There was no need to wait longer, or see more.

Falling back into the woods, Bascom turned and raced toward his horse. He cursed himself for the fact that he'd been right, that Luther Hall had caught him out. He told himself that the easy way hadn't worked, and now there was nothing left but the other way. The hard way.

Jordan jumped from behind a tree into the buckskin's path. Startled, Bascom hauled back on the reins and brought his horse to a skidding halt. The buckskin went wall-eyed with fright and Jordan grabbed the halter. He put a finger to his mouth, silencing Bascom, and led them into a grove of timber.

The roan gelding, Homer, and the longhorn heifer were tied to separate trees. The bull was stamping and pawing, pulling back on the rope, clearly disgruntled that his tree was too far removed from the heifer's tree. Bascom swung down out of the saddle, thoroughly confused. He glared at Jordan.

"What the hell's the matter? Why do you keep shushing me?"

"Hold it down," Jordan said, jerking his thumb in a rapid gesture. "There's Comanche up there, just got a quick look."

Bascom's mouth dropped open. "Comanche?"

"Whole bunch, eight or nine at least. The creek ends up there aways, spring-fed like we thought. I saw a little pond."

"What're the Injuns doing up there?"

"Look to be watering their ponies," Jordan said, still whispering. "Probably just a hunting party, but I didn't hang around to find out. We're on their reservation, and they don't look any too tame. Like you said before, a stray white man could still lose his scalp."

"Holy Jesus!" Bascom croaked. "Our fat's in the fire now."

"What're you talkin' about?"

"I'm talkin' about Dolan and his band of skunks. Spotted them downstream and took off like a scalded cat. They'll be here any minute."

"Kiss my ass!" Jordan said brusquely. "Dolan on one side and Comanche on the other. Got any bright ideas?"

Bascom looked stumped. "Damned sure no place to run. We'll have to hunker down and hope nobody spots us." He spat tobacco juice, glancing around at the trees. "Pretty skimpy cover for all we've got to hide."

"Too late to move now. We'll just have to hold

our breath and see what happens. Maybe Dolan and his boys will stumble on the Comanches."

"That'd sure solve a heap of problems."

Jordan's gaze went past his shoulder. "Newt, you'd better unlimber your rifle. Here they come."

Bascom turned, saw the five riders not fifty yards downstream. Through the scattered trees, he made out Luther Hall in the lead. He pulled his rifle from the scabbard, and a moment later, Jordan took a position behind a nearby tree, rifle in hand. They waited as the riders moved forward along the creek.

Homer suddenly reared back against his lead rope. He cast a forlorn look at the brindle heifer and raised his snout to the sky. His mouth opened and he bellowed a roar of frustration and unrewarded yearning. The sound blasted through the woods like a bugle call.

Luther Hall stopped, his gaze drawn to the grove of trees. Then, as though reverting to an ancient time, his voice raised in a gobbled war cry. He spurred his horse, and thundered forward, dodging and weaving through the scattered timber. He pulled his pistol, firing as he charged forward.

To the rear, Dolan and the other men appeared momentarily at a loss. But then, following the direction of Hall's charge, they spotted Jordan and Bascom. Their horses spooked at the crack of gunfire, and they fought to bring them under control. Hall was halfway through the stand of trees before they got themselves straightened out. Dolan jerked his pistol, motioning them onward.

Jordan shouldered his rifle. He tracked Dolan through the trees and fired, cursing when he missed. He worked the lever on the Winchester, loosing a rapid volley of shots, forcing the gang to scatter along the creek. Off to his side, Bascom stood stock-still, the rifle-butt tucked into his shoulder. Slugs ripped past, skinning bark off trees, but he waited until he had a clear shot at Hall. When he fired, the half-breed was blown backward out of his saddle and tumbled headfirst to the ground. The muzzle blast from Bascom's rifle turned the horse and set him galloping back toward the creek.

Off to the south, where the terrain rose to the spring-fed pond, the Comanche braves suddenly boiled over the rise. Jordan's rifle went dry as they appeared, and Bascom withheld fire. The Comanches thundered past, unaware of Jordan and Bascom hidden in the grove of trees. Their attention was instead centered on the four white men alongside the creek. Whooping war cries, joyous at the prospect of tangling with white-eyes who had invaded their land, the braves charged down the slope. Some opened fire with rifles and others loosed a shower of steel-tipped arrows.

Dolan and his gang broke before the charge. They slewed their horses around, turning downstream in a headlong gallop. Arnie Grove fell first, an arrow buried between his shoulder blades. Then, scarcely an instant later, a rifle slug knocked Jack Langham off his horse. One brave, then another, leaped off their ponies, scalping knives in hand. Ahead, bent low in the saddle, Dolan and Buster Fenton rode for their lives. The Comanches pounded after them in hot pursuit.

Jordan looked on with a bemused expression. He finally turned to Bascom. "What d'you think of that, Newt?"

"I think we'd better get while the gettin's good."

"I'm with you, pardner. Let's make tracks."

# TWENTY-FIVE

Three days later, they sighted Palo Duro Canyon. After crossing the line from Indian Territory, they had turned southwest across the open plains. The Panhandle looked not only inviting, but curiously peaceful. Something about being on home ground lifted their spirits.

A full day and part of a night had been required for the last leg of their journey through Indian Territory. Bascom was in a constant state of vigilance, and Jordan had grown more cautious as well. The sight of Comanches, with their warrior blood rekindled, was enough to put any man on guard. Upon nearing the headwater of the Washita, they finally knew they'd crossed the line. Only at that point had they stopped looking over their shoulders.

The great fissure of Palo Duro loomed ahead. Neither of them had spoken in a long while; they were lost in their own thoughts. But now, with their assignment nearly ended, Bascom broke the silence. He looked concerned.

"We gotta decide something pretty quick. I'm talkin' about that dustup with the Comanches."

Jordan lit a fresh-rolled cigarette. "What about it?"

"Thing is," Bascom said, "do we tell the truth and get ourselves branded as liars? Or do we lie and make it sound like the truth?"

"Newt, what the hell are you talkin' about?"

"You think anybody's gonna believe a word of it? How the redsticks saved our butts and took scalps? Sounds like one of them tall tales Buffalo Bill fobs off on newspaper reporters."

"C'mon," Jordan said, exhaling smoke. "Everybody knows Bill Cody don't mean no harm. Just pleasures him to go around spinnin' windies."

"That's my point," Bascom came back. "You wanna get a reputation for blowin' hot air? Folks might never believe another word we said."

"Well, Newt, it's a helluva story. Who else you know that the Comanche rode to their rescue?"

"Not one livin' soul! Seems funny we'd be the first, don't it?"

Jordan nodded. "Still a helluva story."

"So what?" Bascom said. "Try tellin' it in the bunkhouse and see what happens. The boys would laugh us out the door."

"Yeah, maybe you're right."

"Gawddamn right I'm right. We'd never live it down."

"So how do we explain how we got away from Dolan and his bunch?"

"Just say we outfoxed 'em back at the creek. Folks'll think we're real clever sonsabitches."

Jordan laughed. "Couple of stalwart detectives, huh?"

"Why not?" Bascom rejoined. "We got the job done, didn't we? Let that speak for itself."

"Now that you mention it, I wish we had finished the job. Troubles me that I missed Dolan there at the last. Thought I had him dead center in my sights."

"No need to fret yourself. His hair's hangin' in some Comanche lodge right now. Probably cure out real nice."

"All the same," Jordan said. "I'd sooner have shot him myself. Gettin' scalped is a hard way to go."

"Look at it thisaway," Bascom said, jerking a thumb over his shoulder. "We got Homer back home safe and sound. Nothin' else counts."

Homer trailed along behind on the lead rope. By now, he and the brindle heifer were intimate traveling companions. Homer stuck to her as though he'd forsworn a harem of cows for the bliss of monogamy. The heifer, in turn, clung to him like she'd found a king among kings. They appeared mated for life.

Jordan led the way down the narrow trail along the north wall of Palo Duro Canyon. The heifer was next in line, followed closely by an ever-protective Homer. Bascom brought up the rear as they moved steadily down the rocky path. A blazing noonday sun marked their passage onto the canyon floor.

An hour later they reined to a halt at the Circle I compound. As they dismounted by the corral, Lord Stanley Ingram emerged from the main house. For a moment, as if struck immobile by shock, he stood

on the porch staring at them with wide-eyed disbelief. Then, his gangly legs pumping, he stepped off
the porch and hurried forward. His face split in a
broad, toothy grin.

"Homer!" he shouted, ignoring the men. "You're
home, old fella. You've come back!"

"In the flesh," Bascom said proudly. "No worse
for wear either."

Ingram looked as though he were about to kiss
the bull. One arm still locked about Homer's neck,
he glanced around. "Gentlemen!" he said joyously.
"How can I ever thank you? I'm in your debt for
life."

"Forget it," Jordan said. "We're glad things
worked out awright."

"Everyone has given you up for lost. Over a
month now and no word at all. Quite frankly, we
thought the worst—that you'd been killed."

Bascom splattered a corral post with tobacco
juice. "We come close a couple of times," he said,
trying for an offhand tone. "Found Homer over in
Indian Territory. The bunch that stole him wasn't
too keen on lettin' go."

"I must hear the story—" Ingram suddenly
stopped, staring at the altered brand. "What on earth
is that?"

"Thieves' work," Jordan informed him. "They
have to doctor the brand in order to sell rustled
stock. Changed it from Circle I to Circle Three."

"The brigands!" Ingram cursed roundly. "Bloody
rotters deserve to be drawn and quartered!"

"Fact is—" Jordan got a warning look from Bascom. "Well, the way it worked out," he went on, "they won't be rustlin' any more stock. Unless it's in the Happy Hunting Ground."

"I beg your pardon?"

"What he means," Bascom cut in, "we put 'em out of business. All washed up."

"Jolly good show," Ingram said cheerily. He paused, abruptly aware of the heifer cuddled close to Homer. "Where did this longhorn come from? She's not wearing my brand."

Bascom gave him a brief explanation. "What you've got here," he concluded, "are a couple of lovebirds. Homer can't bear to have her outta his sight."

"Indeed?" Ingram fondly patted the bull. "Have no fear, Homer. Your friend shall have the stall next to your own." He turned back to the detectives. "You gentlemen have done a commendable job, absolutely marvelous. I insist on rewarding you somehow."

"No need," Jordan said. "We was just doing our job."

"Your modesty becomes you, Mr. Jordan. However, I daresay your efforts deserve—" He suddenly stopped, struck by random inspiration. "Yes, of course! The very thing."

Ingram quickly marched them up to the house. Inside, he led them directly to his study. He halted, one arm flung out in a dramatic pose, indicating the painting over the mantlepiece. His smile was one of noblesse oblige, the grand gesture of an aristocrat.

"I insist that you accept this painting as a small token of my gratitude."

Jordan and Bascom stared at the painting of Homer. They traded a perplexed glance, and then Jordan gently shook his head. "Lord Ingram, we appreciate the offer. We surely do. But we couldn't ask you to part—"

"Nonsense!" Ingram interrupted. "Homer would concur that it is only proper. Who else more richly deserves his portrait than you? The men who returned him safely from God knows what fate!"

With the offer so eloquently phrased, there was no way to refuse. Ingram then asked for a full account of their grand adventure in Indian Territory. When they begged off, pleading exhaustion, he extracted a promise that they would return another time. A short while later they rode out with the framed painting. Bascom got the chore of juggling it from horseback.

Once again on the tableland above Palo Duro, they turned north. Bascom rode tilted in the saddle, the painting clutched tightly under one arm. He struggled not to let the gilt-edged frame drag the ground. Finally, his tone exasperated, he looked over at Jordan.

"We're gonna get ragged out of the bunkhouse. The boys won't never let us hear the end of this."

"Newt, you're lookin' at it all wrong."

"How so?"

"What do people call us—our nickname?"

"You know that as well as me. The Durham Brothers."

"So called," Jordan said, "because I smoke it and you chew it. Right?"

"Yeah, right," Bascom muttered. "So what's your point?"

"We're gonna hang that painting over our bunks. Let it stand as a testimonial as to how we saved Homer, and a reminder about our tobacco of choice, Bull Durham. Hell, before the night's out, you'll probably have a lecture that tells the whole story. Wouldn't doubt but what the boys will pay admission to hear you talk."

Bascom worked his cud a moment, thoughtful. "You know, you might have something there. Christ, it all blends together, don't it? Our savin' Homer, and Bull Durham, and the Durham Brothers." He chuckled to himself. "We're just liable to wind up legends."

"That's the ticket," Jordan said jovially. "I might just pay admission to hear it myself."

"Not tonight you won't. After supper, I'm headed for Tascosa. Gonna play some poker and sip a little whiskey. Let the wolf howl!"

"Guess I'll swing by Rebecca's place and tell her I'm home. That'll give her time to get all fixed up for tonight—when I come callin'."

"Figgered as much," Bascom said with a sly smile. "Long as you've been gone, she'll likely love you to death. Careful you don't let her cripple you."

"Newt, you always did have a dirty mind."

"Ol' ring-dang-doo, she'll get you every time!"

They parted a short time later. Jordan turned northeast, toward the Culpepper ranch. Bascom, juggling the painting, rode toward the Bar B. He was still chuckling to himself.

• • •

Jordan dismounted outside the house. He left his horse at the hitch rack and started across the yard. At the last moment, he removed his hat and swatted trail dust off his clothes. He wondered if he looked as grungy as he felt.

Nearing the porch, he heard women's voices from inside. One he pegged as Rebecca and the second, considerably louder, was the mother. From the sound of it, they were involved in a heated discussion. Naomi Culpepper, as usual, got the last word.

"Don't be a ninny! Tell him and have it done with!"

Rebecca moved through the door onto the porch. Her cheeks were flushed an apple-red and she appeared somewhat disconcerted. She walked to the edge of the porch, hands clasped behind her back. Her dimples tweaked in a nervous smile.

"Hello, Sam."

Jordan's voice failed him. From the mother's parting remark, and the girl's rattled manner, he knew what was coming. He'd been gone a full cycle of the moon, every girl's nightmare when she was fooling around. He sensed that Rebecca was about to tell him she was in a family way. He finally managed a strangled greeting.

"Hello there, Becky. You're lookin' real pretty."

"I feel terrible." She dropped her eyes, avoiding his gaze. "Sam, I've got some awful news."

"Oh?" Jordan felt a loud ringing in his ears. "What's that?"

"You stayed away too long this time, Sam. You shouldn't have left me alone and . . . and nowhere to turn."

"Becky, I'm not followin' you."

"What I'm trying to tell you, without hurting your feelings . . ." She faltered, shifting from foot to foot. "I've been keeping company with Tom Pryor. We're betrothed, Sam. He proposed just last week."

Jordan found himself able to breathe again. The news was bad, but good! She wasn't in a family way, not by him anyhow. He nodded, trying to hide the sudden elation behind a humble tone.

"Don't blame yourself, Becky. I'm the one at fault."

"God, Sam!" Her voice trembled. "Tom's fixing to quit the Slash O and come to work for Daddy. Mama kept after me and after me"—her eyes glistened—"and finally I just said 'yes.' "

"Tom Pryor's a hard worker. He'll make you a good husband, Becky. I wish you all the best."

"Lord in heaven, why didn't you ever ask me, Sam?"

"Just fiddle-footed, I suppose. Not much of an excuse—"

She turned and fled back into the house. Jordan walked back to his horse, stepped into the saddle. He reined away and put the roan into a steady lope. Somehow, he thought his conscience ought to be bothering him. But he felt good, riding into the wind, a free man. The words joined together in his head and he laughed aloud. Free as the wind.

. . .

An hour later he slammed through the door of the bunkhouse. Bascom stood before their bunks, admiring the painting of Homer, which was now mounted on the wall. Several cowhands were seated around the room, watching Bascom with bemused expressions. They turned as the door popped shut.

"Newt," Jordan said, striding across the room. "I'm glad you haven't gone yet."

Bascom looked him over. "What the hell's with you? You got a funny light in your eyes."

"I'm celebratin'," Jordan said. "The job's done and we're back home—and I'm not gettin' married."

"No joke?" Bascom said. "You've cut the cord, have you?"

"Cut the cord and fixin' to cut the wolf loose. Let's head for Tascosa."

Bascom grinned. "Well, kiss my dusty butt!"

"No, thank you, Newt. But I'll buy the first drink."

"What're we waitin' on, then?"

"Hell, we're not waitin'. Let's ride!"

# TWENTY-SIX

"Y ou're joshin' me!"

"Honest to God's truth, Newt."

"Why would anybody marry Tom Pryor? That blubbergut don't know his ass from his elbow."

Pryor was the cowhand who had started a fight the last time they'd visited the saloon in Tascosa. Bascom still remembered how Pryor had overturned the card table and busted him in the nose. Though he'd won the fight, he hadn't forgiven Pryor for being a sore loser.

"Tell you one thing," Bascom went on. "The game of poker gives you a pretty good gauge of a man's character. Far as I'm concerned, Tom Pryor ain't got none."

Dusk was settling over the plains. Earlier, they'd made their report to Alex Blalock, president of the Cattlemen's Association. Then, after accepting his congratulations, they started out for the evening's celebration. Oncoming darkness found them still some five miles from Tascosa.

Jordan lit a cigarette now, thinking of Bascom's

remark on Tom Pryor. He exhaled, his words framed in smoke. "I tend to doubt the Culpeppers ever took Pryor's character into account."

"Why's that?"

"They're just interested in marryin' the girl off. Practically any damn fool would do, so long as he takes her off their hands."

"Helluva note," Bascom said. " 'Course, they're liable to get more'n they bargained for."

"How so?"

"Well, you said Pryor's quittin' the Slash O to work for Culpepper. Knowin' Pryor, he probably figgers he found himself a gravy train."

"Yeah, I could see that," Jordan observed. "Once they're married, and he gets Becky in a family way, the Culpeppers couldn't hardly run him off. He could loaf around, just work when he felt like it."

"Lives long enough," Bascom added, in a mock serious tone, "he'll wind up inheriting the ranch. You shore missed the boat there, Sam. You could've had Becky, and a passel of kids, and the Culpepper spread. You'd have been set for life."

Jordan knew he was being ribbed. He went along with the joke. "You know, maybe I could still bring Becky around. Get her to ditch Pryor and take me back."

Bascom almost swallowed his chaw. "Whoa there, hoss! I was just funnin' you. Don't do nothin' you'll regret."

"Well, you'll have to admit, it's a pretty cushy proposition."

"Bunch of snot-nosed kids and a fat wife? I don't see you settlin' down to the likes of that."

"Guess you're right," Jordan said, a note of feigned reluctance in his voice. "Never could abide small children in large numbers. And Becky's powerful set on havin' lots of kids. At least a dozen."

"Twelve kids!" Bascom sputtered. "Holy jumpin' Jesus! You'd have gone batty in no time."

"Way it worked out, I reckon I got lucky. Off chasin' Homer kept us away just long enough for Tom Pryor to slip in the back door."

"Figger it that way, you're sorta in his debt. We oughta buy him a drink next time he comes around."

"Good idea," Jordan agreed. "I sure enough owe him one."

"'Course, you understand," Bascom said hurriedly, "that don't change my opinion of the sorry sonovabitch. I still won't never play cards with him again."

"Newt, I just suspect he'll never ask."

Some while later they rode into Tascosa. Out front of the saloon, they dismounted and tied their horses to the hitch rack. When they entered the door, they were surprised to find the saloon empty. Joe Tate stood behind the bar, thumbing through a dog-eared copy of the *Police Gazette*.

"Well, looky here," he said. "Where'd you boys spring from?"

"Got in today," Bascom said, glaring around at the empty room. "Where's everybody at? I planned on gettin' a poker game started."

"Most everybody's flat broke and nursing a hangover. We just celebrated Independence Day last Saturday."

Bascom glanced at the calendar tacked to the wall. The date was July 10. "Jesus," he muttered. "We've been gone longer than I thought."

"Damned if you haven't," Tate said. "Lots of folks thought you was dead and buried by now. Where you been?"

"Got delayed over in Indian Territory."

"How'd it go? You locate Ingram's fancy bull?"

"Shore did," Bascom said, pride in his voice. "Brought him back fit as a fiddle. Just dropped him off this afternoon."

"You don't say! Well, boys, that calls for a round on the house."

Tate set three glasses and a bottle of rye on the counter. He poured, then raised his glass in a toast. "Glad to see you boys all in one piece. Happy days."

They downed the shots, and Bascom smacked his lips in appreciation. Jordan pulled out the makings and creased a paper. He glanced at Tate, struck by a wayward thought. "Joe, have you ever seen a Durham bull? Like the one we brought back?"

"Can't say as I have."

Jordan held out the muslin bag. "Looks just like the one on that Bull Durham sack. Fact is, that's how the tobacco got its name. Used a Durham bull on the label."

Tate studied the label. "Don't look much like a longhorn, does he?"

"Nope." Jordan finished rolling his cigarette and

lit up. "'Course, there's a world of difference between the two. A purebred Durham will cost you about five thousand."

"Dollars?" Tate said in wonderment. "You brought back a five-thousand-dollar bull?"

"Yeah, we surely did."

"Hope you got yourselves a proper reward."

Bascom grinned. "Lord Ingram treated us real good. No complaints a'tall."

"By golly," Tate said, pouring a refill. "That calls for another drink."

"Joe, I like your whiskey," Bascom told him, "but liquor don't taste the same without a poker game. You sure nobody's gonna drift by?"

"Hell, Newt, I wish't you'd been here last Saturday. Place was packed to the rafters and everybody tossin' money to the winds. You would've been in hog heaven."

Bascom started to feel depressed. Before he could reply, the door opened, and he looked around, thinking he might get a card game after all. Then, as though he'd seen a ghost, his jaw clicked open. He nudged Jordan.

"You ain't gonna believe who just walked in."

Rafe Dolan and Buster Fenton stood in the doorway. Their clothes were torn and streaked with grime, and Fenton had a bloody kerchief tied around his left arm. Dolan fixed Jordan with a hard stare.

"Before I kill you," he said coldly, "I want to know what you've done with my bull."

"Rafe, you're a sight," Jordan said, aware that

Bascom had moved away from the bar. "How the hell'd you get clear of them Comanches?"

"We outfought 'em and we outrun 'em. Which ain't neither here nor there. Where's my bull?"

"We've got lots of time, if it's killin' you want. Let me ask you a question."

"Stall all you like and it won't change nothin'. Go ahead and ask."

Jordan was genuinely curious. "How'd you find us?"

The tension seemed to melt away from Dolan. He smiled, clearly proud of himself. "That creek you took ran off to the south. Opposite direction from Dodge City."

"So?"

"So I asked myself where you'd hole up with a bull. Figured you wouldn't try Fort Worth, since that'd be the obvious place to look. Only one place left out in these parts."

"Tascosa."

"On the nose," Dolan said, even more pleased with himself. "What you didn't know was that we stole that bull right here in the Panhandle. The joke's on you."

Jordan smiled. "Don't bet on it, Rafe."

"You got your answer and now I'll have mine. Where's the bull?"

"Down at Palo Duro, on the Circle I. Where you stole him."

"Don't gimme that!" Dolan bristled. "You wouldn't take him back there."

"Yeah, I would," Jordan said. "You see, Newt and

me work for the Cattlemen's Association. We're range detectives."

Dolan appeared skeptical. Then he studied Jordan's somber expression, and his doubt wavered. "You're on the level, aren't you?"

"Wouldn't kid you about that, Rafe."

"No, I guess you wouldn't. But you sure made a fool of me back in the Nations. You boys are accomplished liars."

"All part of the job," Jordan said. "Any way we can work this out, Rafe?"

"Like how?"

"Well, you and Fenton could surrender. We'd see to it that you get a fair trial."

"Sure you would," Dolan said bitterly. "And a long stretch in prison."

"There's worse things."

"Nothin' worse than—"

Dolan tried for surprise. The flow of his words was abruptly cut short, and he went for the gun on his hip. He was quick, with no lost motion, and his gun popped out of the holster. But Jordan had seen the trick once before, at Will Musgrave's trading post, and it hadn't fooled him then. Nor was he taken off guard now.

Jordan's arm moved and the Colt appeared in his hand. He fired a split second before Dolan's gun came level, and a starburst of blood splattered the gangleader's chest. Bascom and Buster Fenton were only a beat behind, drawing their guns as the first shot was fired. But Bascom was an instant faster, and deadly accurate. His slug bored through the sternum, exploded Fenton's heart.

Dolan staggered back against the door. His expression was strangely bewildered, as though unable to comprehend that he'd been shot. His arm straightened, and all his concentration focused on bringing the gun level. Jordan thumbed the hammer on his Colt as Buster Fenton collapsed at the knees and slumped to the floor. Staring over the sights, Jordan fired, and Dolan stumbled sideways in a nerveless dance. His eyes went blank and his body went slack. He fell, discharging his gun into the floor, and hit hard on his face. His right leg jerked in a spasm of afterdeath.

Bascom walked forward, checking the bodies. He turned and nodded to Jordan. "They're finished."

"Jesus Christ," Joe Tate murmured, frozen against the back bar. "Why'd he pull on you?"

Jordan smiled. "Rafe Dolan wasn't a quitter. He had to try."

"Yeah, but the dumb bastard got himself killed."

"Well, Joe, like they say, nobody lives forever."


There was no ceremony. Rafe Dolan and Buster Fenton were buried in Tascosa's graveyard the next morning. Jordan and Bascom shoveled dirt into the holes, and marked the graves with crude wooden crosses. Then they rode out of town, toward the Bar B.

Neither of them felt any remorse. Yet they were curiously sobered by the killings. For all this faults, Dolan had been a man of daring and grit. They were bothered not so much by his death, but rather the fact that they'd been forced to kill him. They somehow wished the Comanche had saved them the trouble.

At the ranch, they were summoned up to the main house. Alex Blalock greeted them in his study and waved them to chairs. Jordan began rolling a cigarette, and Blalock examined them with a quizzical expression. He thought they looked off their feed.

"What's the problem?" he asked. "Joe Tate serve you some bad whiskey?"

Jordan struck a match on his thumbnail. "Rafe Dolan showed up last night. We had to kill him."

"How'd he find you?"

"Lucky guess," Jordan said, exhaling smoke. " 'Course, in a way, I suppose you could say his luck ran out."

"I'll be damned," Blalock said, staring at them. "No wonder your reputation's spread so far."

"Our reputation?" Bascom said. "What're you talkin' about?"

Blalock dropped a letter on the desk. "That come in with the supply wagon this morning. Head of the Wyoming Stockgrowers' Association has requested your services. Asked for you by name."

"By name?"

"Sam Jordan and Newt Bascom. Otherwise known as the Durham Brothers. Wants you to take on an undercover assignment."

Bascom perked up. "He say what that means, exactly?"

"Yep," Blalock replied. "Gang of horse thieves operating out of the Hole-in-the-Wall. That's some sort of wilderness hideout."

"Sounds serious." Jordan looked interested. "Question is, can you spare us? Wyoming's a long ways off."

"Way I see it, we've got to cooperate with other associations. Only way we'll ever get rid of the lawless element. I'm willin' to loan you boys out—for one job."

Jordan glanced around. "What do you think, Newt?"

"Hell, why not?" Bascom said, grinning. "Heard tell the High Plains are a sight to behold. Maybe we oughta have ourselves a look-see."

"Suits me," Jordan said, nodding at Blalock. "When do we leave?"

"Today," Blalock said. "They want you up there *muy pronto*."

Shortly after noontime, Jordan and Bascom rode out of the compound. A packhorse trailed behind, loaded with supplies for the long journey to Wyoming. Neither of them knew what lay ahead, but that hardly mattered. They were off to see a new land, the fabled High Plains.

"Ain't that a helluva note," Bascom said, squirting a rock with tobacco juice. "They actually asked for the Durham Brothers. You reckon we're famous, Sam?"

Jordan rolled himself a smoke. He lit up, savoring a long drag. "Tell you what's a fact, Newt. If we're not, I've got a hunch we're gonna be. Wyoming's a mighty rough place."

They rode north toward Hole-in-the-Wall.